MW01255065

STAR STRUCK

Amber Garza

Graphic Designer: Kris @C & K Creations

Other titles by Amber Garza

Head Above Water
Falling to Pieces
Star Struck
Love Struck
Tripping Me Up
Finding Me Again
Winning Me Over
Break Through
Break Free
Cuts Run Deep
Engraved

Delaney's Gift Series:
Dazzle
Shatter
Betray

The Prowl Trilogy
Prowl
Entice
Unveil

To connect with Amber Garza online:
http://www.ambergarza.wordpress.com
https://www.facebook.com/pages/Amber-Garza-author

To anyone who has ever dreamed of being a rockstar

1
Star

I wipe my clammy hands down my jeans. My fingernail snags on a loose thread, and I yank it out. Then bite down on the jagged edge. Lola raises an eyebrow at me, and I quickly retract my fingers from my mouth. Nail biting is a habit I'm trying hard to break now that I'm in college. I glance down at my stubby nails and cringe. I guess I'm not doing a great job.

The girl on stage strums her guitar loudly and belts out a note in a way that makes me wince. Lola flashes me an amused look, but it only succeeds in turning my stomach. I lean forward, resting my elbows on the slick pub table we're seated at. "I can't believe I let you talk me into this."

"Oh, come on. You are a million times better than this girl."

"That's not saying much."

"Trust me, you're gonna blow this place out of the water." Lola plucks the cup of soda off the table and takes a dainty sip. Everything about Lola is dainty from her French manicured nails, to her coifed black hair and her ruby red lipstick. She always reminds me of an actress from the 1950's. I rub my lightly glossed lips together, tuck a strand of my straight brown hair behind my ears, and glance down at my short nails that haven't been painted in years. Maybe I should finally let Lola give me that makeover she's always threatening me with. "You are so much more talented than you give yourself credit for."

That's the reason Lola has been my best friend for so long. She believes in me in a way that no one else does. And she's always encouraging me to put myself out there. Even though it infuriates me sometimes, the truth is, that I'm grateful to her. However, at this moment I'm terrified. We've only been on campus for a week, and she's already talked me into performing at open mic night at a popular coffee shop. The place is jam packed with people, and every time a new person enters the room my insides are attacked by another swarm of angry butterflies.

"Ooh, you're up next," Lola squeals, her eyes dancing with excitement.

Goodie. My palms fill with more moisture and I feel dangerously close to puking. When my name is called, I throw Lola a pained look and force my legs to carry me up on the makeshift stage. Peering down at my long shirt, skinny jeans and ballet flats, I'm grateful that I'm not wearing heels. Since I'm only five foot four, I tend to wear high heels a lot. But judging by how violently my legs are shaking, I'm pretty sure if I weren't wearing my flats I'd be face down on the ground by now. Thankfully I make it to the stage and I plop down at the keyboard. With shaky fingers I pull the microphone to my lips and rest my fingers on the keys. I take a deep breath to steady my nerves, and I don't dare look out at the room. If I just pretend I'm alone in my room singing I should be okay. I love to sing and play. It's probably my favorite thing in the world to do, but performing is something I'm still not comfortable with.

I decide to play a song I wrote a couple of years ago for my ex-boyfriend Spencer. It's one I've sang so many times I could probably sing it in my sleep, so I figure it's a safe bet. Even if I completely blank out I won't forget the lyrics or anything. When I press down on the first key, I close my eyes and allow my mind to drown out the room. I focus on the music, letting the lyrics and notes whisk me away. As I splash around in the waves of the song, eventually I go under, drowning in it.

I want you close
I want you here
I feel complete

When you are near

After playing the last chord, I finally come out of my trance and open my eyes, taking in the room. The first person I notice is Lola, and she's beaming up at me. The room has quieted down and all eyes seem to be on me. This causes my heart to start beating frantically in my chest. I stand up, and a smattering of applause ensues.

Swallowing hard, I take deliberate steps off the stage, keeping my eyes trained on the ground. Before I can reach my table, a guy about my age intercepts me. He has brown hair that falls a little past his ears in a sweep that reminds me of the typical look of the members of boy bands. His eyes are dark and the lines around them crinkle as he smiles at me.

"Hey, you were pretty great up there," he says.

I bite my lip, heat creeping up into my cheeks. "Thanks."

"I'm Ryker." He juts out a hand to mine.

After swiping my sweaty hand over the thigh of my jeans, I hold my hand out too. "Star."

"I like it." He cocks an eyebrow.

"I'm Lola," my friend calls out from where she is seated at our table. "Why don't you join us, Ryker?" Lola indicates the extra chair at our small table.

Ryker smiles as he plops down into the

4

chair. "Don't mind if I do."

I slide into the chair opposite him and glance over at Lola. She's grinning from ear to ear, and I know exactly what she's thinking. It turns my stomach. I'm so not ready to get back in the dating game. I just got out of a two-year relationship, and by that I mean I got dumped big time by the only boy I've ever loved. Honestly, I thought that Spencer was the one. Clearly I was wrong, but the thought of jumping into another relationship right now does not sound appealing.

Lola nudges me and I glance back over at Ryker. I suppose he's pretty cute, but I'm not sure he's really my type. In truth, he looks more like Lola's type with his trendy outfit and hair style that he clearly put a lot of effort into.

The next performer starts playing, so Ryker leans toward me. "I'm in a band and we're looking for a female singer. I think you'd be perfect."

This perks my interest. "Like a lead singer?" I'm not sure I'm ready to be the front runner of a band. I could hardly get through open mic night without emptying the contents of my stomach on stage.

"No, we have a lead singer. We're looking for kind of a backup singer, I guess. But there would be plenty of opportunities to feature one of your songs if you wanted to," Ryker explains.

I shift uncomfortably in my seat. "I don't

know. I've never really been in a band before."

"Why not? You're amazing," Ryker gushes.

Lola elbows me in the side. "I've been telling her that for years."

Ryker peers over at Lola and raises his eyebrows. I recognize that look. Pretty much every guy I meet is attracted to Lola. It's almost impossible not to be. "Smart friend."

"You have no idea," she jokes, running a finger over the rim of her glass.

"Thanks for the offer, Ryker, but I'm just not sure about it." I look to Lola for some help. Surely she won't want me to join a band with a complete stranger. For all I know he could be a serial killer.

"Why don't you give us your information and Star can give you a call to discuss it further?" Lola asks.

Ryker grins, pushing away from the table. "Great. I'll be right back."

I glare at Lola, who just shrugs her shoulders in response.

"I'm not joining his band," I hiss over the loud music blaring from onstage.

"Why not?" Lola runs a long fingernail through her shiny hair.

"I don't know anything about the guy. I don't even know the name of his band. What if he

6

doesn't even have a band?" Panic chokes me at the thought.

Lola just laughs and waves away my words with a graceful flick of her wrist. "Did you see the guy? He screams 'boy band'. But finding out if his story is legit will be easy enough."

I have no idea what she's talking about, but Ryker reappears before I can ask her. He shoves a piece of paper at me. I glance down and see a phone number and address scrawled on it. "Whose address is this?"

"Our lead singer," Ryker says. "We practice in his parents' garage."

Seriously? I am so not showing up at some stranger's house. This is getting even more suspicious. I throw Lola a cautionary look, and she grimaces back. Finally she's on my side.

"We're practicing tomorrow night at seven. You should come and jam with us." Ryker rolls his shoulders.

I open my mouth to tell him no thank you, but I clamp my mouth shut as my gaze takes in the guy walking on the stage. He's quite possibly the best looking guy I've ever seen. Not only that, but he walks with a swagger that causes everyone to stop and take notice. He has a guitar slung over his shoulder. He's wearing skinny jeans, boots and a black short-sleeved shirt that shows off the intricate tattoo that covers one of his arms. His dark hair is short, and when he smiles at the crowd it causes my heart to flip in my chest. He begins playing, and I'm mesmerized. When he opens his mouth to sing, I freeze. His voice is incredible – raspy, yet controlled in a way that most guys can't master. I'm completely entranced with him.

"Who is he?" I breathe, mostly to myself, but Ryker must hear me because he turns in my direction.

"That's Beckett. He's the lead singer in our band. That's why it's called 'Beckett.' He has a bit of an ego." Ryker chuckles lightly before sitting back in his chair.

I exhale and stare up at the stage. This guy is the leader of the band Ryker wants me to join? I sit still during the remainder of Beckett's song, unable to tear my eyes away from him. When he finishes, the crowd erupts into clapping and I turn to Ryker with a smile.

"I'll be there tomorrow night," I say, my mind made up.

Last night I was so certain about this. Of course I think that had everything to do with seeing Beckett up on stage. I've never been so taken with someone at first glance. However, now as I pull up in front of a complete stranger's house I'm having second thoughts. The house is nice and clean with its blue trim and white shuttered windows, and the lawn is well manicured. But that does little to quell my nerves. I've watched enough crime dramas to know that even serial killers live in pretty houses in nice neighborhoods. Besides, this is just Beckett's parents' house. I have no idea what all the guys in the band are like, and that's who I'll be with, and in the garage no less.

"Hey, you gonna stand out here all day?" Ryker walks toward me, his hands shoved into his pockets.

I jump back, wondering where he came from. "Um, no, I just um...you know...wanted to make sure it was the right house. Which I now see that it is."

Ryker flashes me an amused smile and lightly taps me on the arm. "Come on. I'll introduce you to Beckett."

Just the sound of his name causes my pulse to race. Taking a deep breath, I follow behind Ryker. He ambles over to a box built into the house directly next to the garage. After punching in a few numbers on it, the garage door opens loudly. Inside I can see instruments set up - there's a drum set, a keyboard and guitars resting on stands strewn about. Just as I step inside, a door to the house pops open and Beckett walks through it clutching a bottle of water. I've never wanted to be an inanimate object before, but taking in the way his fingers curl around the sweating bottle I feel a sense of jealousy.

"Hey, Ryker." Beckett nods his head in Ryker's direction as the door slams shut behind him. "The other guys are inside getting a drink. They'll be out in a minute."

I shift uncomfortably from one foot to the other. Beckett hasn't even acknowledged my presence, and last I checked I wasn't invisible. It bothers me, and for a minute I wonder if this was a mistake.

"Hey, Beckett." Ryker pats my arm. "This is the girl I was telling you about. The one from last night's open mic night."

Beckett glances over at me with a bored expression that makes my stomach knot. "Yeah, I missed your song, but Ryker hasn't been able to stop talking about it." He steps close to me, and my breath hitches in my throat. "I'm Beckett."

"Star."

Beckett lets out a harsh laugh that startles me. "A little pretentious, don't you think?"

"Excuse me?"

"I just think artists should stick to their real names, that's all."

His words are like a punch to the gut. I glance over at Ryker who gives me a resigned shrug. I wonder if Beckett's always this much of a jerk. "Star is my real name." When I notice the skeptical look on Beckett's face, I add, "My dad's an astronomer. My parents met at a planetarium, and he proposed under the stars. My brother's name is Galileo. It's sort of a theme in our family."I place my hand on my hip in a challenge. "If I had known I'd be interrogated I would have brought my birth certificate."

Beckett sighs. "I've clearly hit a nerve. It just seemed cliche, that's all."

What? No apology? I'm stunned by his lack of remorse.

Two more guys shove through the door and bound into the garage, talking and laughing loudly. Their voices echo and bounce around me. When their gazes land on me, I have the sudden urge to run away. This whole thing was a bad idea.

"So, you gonna show us what you've got, Star?" Beckett raises an eyebrow at me.

I smile, wanting nothing more than to wipe that smug look off of his face. Maybe once he hears me play he will take me more seriously. "I'd love to." I lift my chin and head over to the keyboard. The rest of the band is completely quiet as they watch me. I ignore the insistent banging of my heart in my chest as I sit at the keyboard. After running my moist palms down the thigh of my jeans, I reach up and place my hands on the slick keys. When I peer up, I catch sight of Ryker and he gives me an encouraging nod. I'm not sure what his story is, but I'm grateful to have at least one person on my side. The other two guys look on warily, and Beckett crosses his arms over his chest, the same bored expression cloaking his face.

I inhale sharply and press down on the keys. Closing my eyes, I open my mouth and allow the song to carry me along. After I sing one verse and chorus, I force my eyelids to open and I slide my fingers back down into my lap. I bite my lip and wait for some response. The silence is deafening.

Ryker grins broadly. "See, didn't I tell you she was amazing, Beckett?"

"Yeah, she's not bad." Beckett shrugs.

The air leaves me and I feel deflated. *Not bad?* I seriously do not need to stay here and be insulted by this egomaniac any longer. I'm just about to push away from the keyboard and stalk out of the garage when Beckett swaggers over to me and shoves a piece of paper in my hand.

"Now let's see how well you harmonize." He glances around the room. "You guys stay out for this. This is just going to be me and Star."

I feel dizzy as I snatch the paper from his hand. The thought of singing with him is enough to keep my butt planted on the seat. Remembering the raspy, rich tone from the night before makes me feel giddy. He slings the guitar over his shoulder, and it catches on his shirt lifting it slightly to reveal his naval and the top of his boxers that creep above his sagging jeans. I avert my gaze and feel my face warm.

He looks up at me, his dark eyes piercing mine. "We'll just run the chorus. You can play if you want to, but if you just want to sing that's fine too."

I nod, glancing down at the paper and taking in the chords and lyrics. Reaching up, I touch the keys. Beckett strums his guitar and I watch him press his lips up to the microphone. It makes me want to take back my desire to be the water bottle. Clearly the mic would be a better choice. When he opens his mouth to sing, I shake away the inappropriate thoughts and focus on the music.

The harmony is simple enough, and as I listen to our voices blend together beautifully a warm feeling swirls in my stomach. I can tell that the other guys hear it too, because they nudge each other and exchange smiles and eyebrow raises.

You're just one more thing I can't have
Standing just outside my grasp
But it doesn't really matter
Because good things never last

When we finish, I peer up at Beckett feeling pleased about the performance.

"I'm sorry." Beckett frowns at me, and my

stomach sinks. "I'm just not sure if this is gonna work out. But thanks for stopping by."

I struggle to stand up, my legs rubbery. As I push away from the keyboard with shaky fingers, my knees soften and I fear I'll fall over. I feel like an idiot; like I've made a complete fool of myself. Without saying a word, I pick up my purse, stalk out of the garage and race to my car.

"Wait! Star!" Ryker calls out, his footsteps pounding behind me.

I whip around. Ryker jogs in my direction. From over his shoulder I can see the other band members watching from the open garage. Well, everyone except for Beckett. He's kneeling on the ground, fidgeting with a string on his guitar.

"Why did you even invite me here?" I ask angrily. "Clearly Beckett isn't interested in having a backup singer."

"Look, I'm reallly sorry about how Beckett acted in there." Ryker runs a hand over his perfectly styled hair.

I soften a little at his words. He's not the person I'm mad at anyway. "It's not your fault. Thanks for giving me the opportunity to try out." I unlock the door to my car and reach for the handle.

"Just give it time. I know Beckett will come around."

I shake my head. "No, I don't think that's

going to happen."

"We've been talking about how badly we need another singer for awhile, and everyone thought you did a great job."

I snort. "Well, everyone except for Beckett, and he is the lead singer and the band is named after him. So, I think it's a safe bet that you're new backup singer won't be me." I tug open the door and slide inside. "See ya later, Ryker." Before he can stop me, I slam the door shut and turn on the engine.

Ryker gives me a sad wave, and turns away. As I pull away from the curb I see him walking back to the garage with sagging shoulders. Feeling eyes on me, I gaze into the garage and see Beckett staring directly into my eyes. I shiver from the intensity of his gaze. The look he gives me causes my heart to arrest. He looks like he's sad to see me go, but I know that's not possible. He's the one who practically threw me out. Facing forward, I force myself to just forget about the whole thing. Sure Beckett is hot, but he's a total jerk. Nothing is ever going to happen between us. In fact, I hope I never even see him again. Angry, I press harder on the gas and tear down the street. I'm grateful that I don't have to drive far before the campus comes into view.

I turn the corner and head toward the parking lot, anger still simmering through my veins. After parking in my usual spot, I turn off the car and bolt out into the cold night. I fling my purse over my shoulder and hug myself as I run toward the dorms, my heels clicking on the pavement.

When I step inside my dorm room I find Lola sitting cross legged on her bed, an open notebook in her lap. She's bent over it scrawling in it with a black pen. Her head jerks up when I slam the door closed. She pushes her hair out of her face, and smiles. "So, are you officially a member of Beckett?"

I shake my head, too mad to speak. Flinging my purse on my bed, I slump down onto it as well. The mattress slumps beneath my weight.

"What happened?" Lola slides the notebook off her lap and sits forward, allowing her legs to dangle off the side of the bed. She's wearing sweat pants and a t-shirt but she still looks stylish somehow.

I groan in frustration, running a hand over my face. "Beckett happened."

"Uh-oh." Lola purses her shiny red lips. "Was sexy rocker boy scared you're gonna steal his spotlight?"

"What?" I crease my forehead in confusion.

"Oh, come on. I saw the guy. He thinks he's God's gift to music. I'm sure once he heard how super talented you are he got scared. He doesn't need his backup singer to upstage him."

As sweet as Lola's words are, they don't ring true. "No, trust me, he didn't seem very impressed with me."

"I'm still going with my theory."

"That's why I love you so much." I smile. "You should have seen how rude he was. How can someone that hot outside be so ugly on the inside?"

"Seriously?" Lola's dark eyes bug out. "When it comes to guys, it's the hot ones I'm wary of. They're usually the biggest jerks."

"Yeah, I guess." I sigh, scooting back on my bed and pulling my bent legs up closer to my body. "I was just hoping Beckett would be different. Besides, it was kind of fun tonight when we sang together. It would have been nice to make it a regular thing."

"What about Ryker?" Lola asks.

"What about him?"

She shrugs. "Well, I mean, he's cute, and he seemed really nice."

Noticing the slight flush of her cheeks, I cock an eyebrow. "Lola, are you crushing on Ryker?"

"That depends." She leans forward, resting her elbows on her knees.

"On what?"

"On how you feel about him?"

17

I swat away her words. "No, go for him. I'm not attracted to Ryker. I mean, he seems like a nice guy, but he's not really my type."

"Not like Beckett, huh?"

My chest tightens when she says his name. I remember how sexy he looked when he sang, and it turns my stomach. "I'm not into Beckett either." When I catch Lola raising her eyebrows at me I add, "At least, not anymore."

"If you say so." Lola flashes me a wicked grin.

"I'm not." I stand up, feeling defensive. "He was arrogant and rude tonight. If I ever see him again it'll be too soon."

"Okay, I believe you." Lola throws up her palms. "But you can't let him stop you from pursuing your music. There's got to be another band you can join."

I roll my eyes, heading toward my dresser. "That's my Lola. Always meddling." I yank open the top drawer and snatch out my fuzzy pajama top and pants.

"I'm serious."

"I didn't even really want to join a band." I whirl around, clutching the clothes to my chest.

"But you just said that it was fun."

I lean my back against the dresser. "It was." My mind flies back to those few blissful moments when Beckett and I were singing together. It was

18

a rush, and the truth is, I'd give anything to experience it again.

"Then what's the issue? You're a musician, aren't you?"

I nod, biting my lip. "Yeah. I guess if it's meant to be it'll happen at some point." My stomach sinks when I'm reminded that it won't be with Beckett. I'm not sure I want to be in any other band. Even though I can't stand Beckett, he is super talented, and it would have been amazing to be part of his band. I try not to let disappointment overwhelm me at the thought. In fact, I try not to think about tonight at all. The whole thing is too depressing and humiliating to relive, even in my mind.

2

Beckett

The girl looks nothing like I expected. When Ryker described her to me I pictured some edgy rocker chick, not some fresh faced girl next door. She wears jeans and sandals, her brown hair sleek down her back. Her skin is soft and smooth with almost no makeup covering it. She smiles up at me with glossy lips, her caramel colored eyes piercing mine. There is so much trust and openness in them that I glance away, unnerved.

When she tells me her name is Star, I can't help myself. I have to give her shit about it. From Ryker's expression I can tell that he doesn't appreciate it, but I don't care. Obviously he's into her, but that's not my problem. Besides, I'm used to Ryker being irritated with me. What I'm not prepared for is Star's reaction. When she lights into me about her name, I wonder if I've misjudged her. Clearly she's got some fire underneath that sweet exterior.

I decide that the least I can do is give her a

shot. Even though I'm pissed at Ryker for springing her on me like this, I shouldn't take it out on her. So, I let her sing for us. I lean back against the wall with my arms across my chest as she sits at the keyboard. Her dark hair falls over her shoulders and her lips purse as her fingertips skim over the keys. When she opens her mouth to sing, I'm surprised with the richness of her tone. As she continues on with the sickeningly sweet song, I figure out why she makes me so uncomfortable. The realization smacks me hard in the gut, and I worry I might throw up. The familiarity of this girl is almost too much. I can't believe I didn't see it before. A thousand unwanted memories assault me and I struggle under the weight of them. As she finishes the song I will the thoughts away, and force myself to calm down.

The minute Star ends the song Ryker peers over at me with that "I told you so" look I hate so much. "See, didn't I tell you she was amazing, Beckett?"

"Yeah, she's not bad," I shoot back. But when I glance back at Star, I see her face fall and then I feel guilty. The comment was more for Ryker's benefit. Even though I want nothing more than to get rid of this girl who bears a haunting resemblance to my past, I don't want to be rude. So with a sigh, I grab a piece of sheet music and walk toward Star. "Now let's see how well you harmonize."

She takes the paper from my fingers, her gaze lingering on my face for a minute. I can see what Ryker sees in her. Her beauty is so natural and pure, very unlike the girls we meet at our shows, which is just another reason I can't let her join the band. This life will eat her alive.

I glance around the room. "You guys stay out for this. This is just going to be me and Star." As I walk back to my guitar, I try not to notice the slight flush of Star's cheeks or the way her eyes light up at my words.

I strum my guitar and start to sing. When I get to the chorus, I can hear Star's voice mingle with mine.

You're just one more thing I can't have
Standing just outside my grasp
But it doesn't really matter
Because good things never last

Our voices blend perfectly, weaving in and out of each other like we were meant to sing together. I shift uncomfortably, pulling the strap of my guitar away from my neck. I feel like I'm being strangled. I just can't do this. There's no way this girl can join our band.

"I'm sorry," I say to her. "I'm just not sure if this is gonna work out. But thanks for stopping by." Then I turn away so I don't have to see the disappointed look in her eyes. After she races out of the garage, Ryker turns to me with a glare.

"What?" I dare Ryker to tell me what he's thinking.

But he doesn't respond. Instead, he just shakes his head and takes off after the girl. Man, he really must want to get in that chick's pants. The other guys share a disgusted look, causing me to grunt and turn away. It's not like I meant to hurt the girl's feelings. The whole thing was Ryker's fault. He had to know how this would end when he brought her here. I glance up to see Star jump into her vehicle and turn on the engine. As she pulls away from the curb, her gaze locks with mine. Her face brings back another unwelcome recollection, and a wave of emotion crashes over me. As she drives away, I know I did the right thing. I may not have been able to save the girl who meant everything to me once upon a time, but at least I can save this one. Maybe this is some sort of redemption.

As Ryker stalks back into the garage, I think about what a silly thought that is. Redemption isn't real. We don't get to right our wrongs that way. If only things were that simple.

"What's with you, man?" Ryker towers over me, his eyes dark. "She was amazing, and you totally shot her down. Is your ego really that fragile?"

Anger sparks. "This has nothing to do with

my ego and you know it." I take a step forward practically bumping Ryker with my chest.

"Okay, calm down you guys," Our electric guitar player Pierce says, moving away from his instrument. Both he and our drummer Jimmy head in our direction.

I back off, nodding to them. "Everything's fine." You'd think Jimmy and Pierce would be used to Ryker and me getting into arguments. Ryker is like a brother to me. We've been friends since we were kids, and we fight just like siblings.

"Is it because she's not the kind of girl you're into?"

"You know that's not why, Ryker." I cock my head to the side, irritated that he's making me say it. "You don't think Star resembles someone else? Someone close to me?"

Ryker furrows his brows in a look of confusion. "What are you talking about?"

I open my mouth ready to the say the name when Ryker's eyes spring open in understanding.

"She doesn't look exactly like her," he says, using an apologetic tone. "There's just a slight resemblance."

"Slight resemblance?"

"Yeah, they both have brown hair and eyes, but that's about it."

"That's not it, Ryker. She's just like Quinn." I can hear the slight intake of breath on

Ryker's part, and I know he's surprised when I say her name. I don't mention her that often. Only when it's necessary. "And that's why she's not joining our band."

"That's what this is about? C'mon, man, she's not Quinn. She's not going to make the same mistakes as her."

"You don't know that." I run my hand through my hair and release a rush of air through gritted teeth. "She was innocent just like her. You might be okay with tainting her, but I'm not."

"We're not tainting anyone. We're just playing music." Ryker laughs bitterly. "Dude, we're the tamest band around. And you saw her, man. She's talented. If we don't pick her up another band will. And I bet they'll mess her up a lot worse than we will."

I mull over his words.

"What if she's picked up by Cold Fever?"

Pierce and Jimmy freeze. My insides coil into knots. I narrow my eyes at Ryker. "You really want her in the band, don't you?"

He nods.

"You must if you brought up those losers." I swallow hard. "Fine. She can join, but she's your responsibility. If anything goes wrong, it's on your head."

Ryker smiles like he just won the stinking lottery. I turn around and prepare to clean up my stuff. My stomach churns, and I wonder if my decision just sealed yet another person's fate.

3
Star

I walk with clipped strides through the campus, my backpack thumping against my shoulder blades. The heavy books inside jostle around, and their sharp edges jab me every once in awhile. It's Monday morning and I'm so not looking forward to the hours of lectures ahead of me. As I round a corner, I bump shoulders with a boy racing past. Without bothering to look up, I adjust the strap of my backpack.

"Star?" a familiar voice says.

I peer up at him. "Hey, Ryker."

"I'm glad I ran into you," he says, and then adds with a laugh, "literally."

I smile, just as my phone buzzes in my pocket. Even though I know it'll be a text from Lola, I still snatch it out and glance down to see what it says.

Maid report: Bed made.

I glance up at Ryker and give him an apologetic face. "Just give me a minute." Then I quickly text back. **Sorry. I thought I did better. At least I picked up my clothes from the floor.**

True. Her response comes almost immediately, and then I push my phone back into my pocket. Lola is a complete neat freak, and I'm kind of a slob. When we first moved in together I feared that it would become a problem for us. Instead, Lola has turned it into a daily joke of maid reports in the form of texts. At least I think it's a joke. I choose to look at them that way, but in truth they have caused me to make more of an effort. However, even with all the effort in the world I will never be as organized as Lola. My creative brain just doesn't work that way.

"I wanted to apologize again for last night," Ryker says.

"It's fine, really. You don't have to keep saying you're sorry. Sometimes these things just don't work out."

"But that's just it. I think it will work out."

I freeze, not wanting him to continue. The last thing I need is false hope about this whole band thing. Why can't Ryker just let it go? I'm never going to humiliate myself like that again. "I think Beckett made it pretty clear that it won't. But thanks anyway." I walk around him.

"Wait." Ryker stops me. "We talked about it after you left last night and we all agreed that you'd make a great addition.

I shake my head. "That's very sweet, but I don't think so."

"C'mon. Please? Beckett feels really bad about his reaction. He honestly did think you were talented."

"Really? Well, then why didn't he say that?"

"Beckett's just complicated, but he's not that bad when you get to know him."

"Well I'm not interested in getting to know him. I think I found out enough last night," I say. "I'm sorry, but I can't put myself through that again. Now if you'll excuse me, I really have to get to class." Without another word, I walk briskly away from Ryker. But no matter how fast I walk, I can't get his words out of my head. Is it true that Beckett did feel bad about his behavior? Did he really think I was talented? As swiftly as the questions enter my mind, I remember the bored look on Beckett's face and the way he dismissed me without any guilt. What is it about him that gets under my skin so bad? I know that the smart thing for me to do right now is just to forget about Beckett and his band; just forget about the whole thing.

"That was super good." Lola links arms with me as we exit the pub we just had dinner in. The cool air circles us as we step outside, and my loose shirt billows around my body. I shiver, goosebumps rising on my flesh. My heels click on the pavement as we walk.

"I know. Fried food is my nemesis." My stomach hurts from the exorbitant amount of fish and chips I just ate.

The dark night sky swallows us, with only the dim light of the streetlamps to direct us to our car. A few vehicles pass by, their tires rumbling on the asphalt. Lola's fruity scent lingers on the slight breeze. We pass by a little club, music spilling outside from the door that is slightly ajar. A couple stands against the window puffing on a cigarette. I bat away the plumes of smoke that reach for me as we walk by. The drumbeat from the club resonates under my feet. When we reach the door, a male's voice sings out, and I freeze.

"What?" Lola halts, raising her eyebrows at me.

I knit my brows together. "I think that's Beckett."

"So?" Lola flashes me a dumbfounded look.

Shrugging, I wriggle my arm out of Lola's grasp move toward the door. I peek inside the club and my heart stops. Beckett is standing on a stage, his eyes closed, his mouth up to a mic and his hands strumming his guitar. Before I can register what I'm doing, I press the door open.

Lola grabs my arm. "I thought you never wanted to see him again."

I bite my lip, knowing she's right. The pull I feel toward Beckett isn't healthy. I should turn around right now and get the hell out of here. Only, for some sick reason I want to stay and listen to him sing. "Just one song?"

Lola heaves a resigned sigh. "Fine."

We push through the crowd and find a small table that is empty near the stage. I slide into one of the chairs, bumping my knees against the bottom of the round table. Lola scoots in next to me. Not until we're seated do I notice just how close to Beckett we are. We're practically sitting on the stage. My palms clam up at the realization. This is probably a mistake. Just when I'm about to hightail it out of here, Beckett looks up and his eyes lock with mine. The look he gives me causes my heart to stutter. It's almost like he's happy to see me. In fact, his lips curl upward into a grin. I suck in a breath, and he lowers his gaze. He continues to sing, and I wonder if I imagined the whole thing. When the song ends his gaze finds me again, and this time there's no mistaking it. Our eyes meet, and he flashes me a crooked grin.

"For this next song I'd like to bring up a very special guest," Beckett speaks in his husky voice that is so sexy I'm sure the entire room is swooning. "We sang this song together earlier in the week, and I'd like to do it again." My stomach drops when he looks pointedly at me. "Star?"

Hearing him say my name causes a rush of chills to skitter down my spine. Lola's mouth drops open, and I'm pretty sure my face looks just as shocked as hers. Glancing up, I catch Ryker's eye from where he stands behind Beckett with his bass guitar in hand. He gives me a subtle nod, and I force my legs to stand. Beckett is wearing an amused grin as I make my way up to the stage. What is he up to? I feel everyone's eyes on me as I take deliberate steps forward, and my face heats up. Once I reach Beckett, panic sweeps over me at the realization that there isn't a keyboard on stage, or even an extra microphone.

As if reading my mind, Beckett curls his index finger beckoning me forward. He holds his microphone between us. My chest tightens. Once I reach him, I stand perfectly still.

"The song is called *Can't Have*." The band starts playing, and I immediately recognize the song as the one I sang with Beckett in his garage. I wipe my sweaty hands on my jeans and dare a look at Lola. She is staring at me with a stunned expression on her face, and it almost causes me to laugh out loud. When I face Beckett again the reality of the situation crashes over me and I worry that I'm about to get sick. He nods at me, stepping closer. We're nearing the chorus. When he faces

32

me, I swallow hard. Our heads are so close together that the microphone is literally the only thing keeping our lips from touching, and it causes me to feel dizzy. I work hard to focus on the lyrics, as I open my mouth and sing in harmony with Beckett.

> *You're just one more thing I can't have*
> *Standing just outside my grasp*
> *But it doesn't really matter*
> *Because good things never last*

As I sing the words, I lose myself in his eyes. I'm so mesmerized it's like the rest of the room fades away and only he and I are standing on this stage. His lips move in sync with mine as our voices mingle together. His fingers close around the microphone between us and his eyes pierce mine. It's one of the most intimate experiences of my life, and when the song ends it takes me a minute to return to reality. When I do, Beckett furrows his brows at me and I wonder how long I continued to stare at him after we finished.

"Thanks for coming," Beckett says to the crowd with a smile. "Good night."

Applause fills the room. Beckett peels off his guitar and sets it down before turning to me. "Thanks for singing with me. I know I caught you off guard."

I am taken aback with how cordial he's

being after our last encounter. However, I'm still not ready to completely let him off the hook. "Sure." I shrug.

"Look, I know I was an ass the other night. It's just that Ryker sprung you on me at the last minute, and I wasn't really prepared." Beckett runs a hand through his hair.

It's not an apology, and I'm starting to wonder if he's even capable of giving one. "Well, maybe you'll be prepared for the next girl who auditions."

"Star," he says in a pleading tone that surprises me. "All the guys in the band thought you were amazing."

"What about you?" I cross my arms over my chest. "What did you think?"

He squirms. "I thought you were good."

I press my lips together, not impressed with his answer. "Good, huh? That's not what you said the other night."

He groans. "I just told you that I wasn't in the mood for an audition the other night. I only wanted to jam, okay?"

Giggling draws my attention away from Beckett. Several girls stand in a cluster by the stage, staring up at Beckett with awed expressions. I roll my eyes.

"Fan club?" I ask.

He glances down at the girls with the same

bored expression he always wears and shrugs. "What can I say? Chicks dig me."

I spin around. This guy's arrogance is so irritating. "Well, thanks for letting me sing with you. Have fun with your fan club."

His hand circles around my wrist. "Wait, Star. You didn't give me an answer."

I turn around slowly, my skin searing from his touch. "You didn't ask me a question."

"Oh, I thought I made myself clear. Are you in or not?"

"In what?" I ask, totally confused.

"The band." He looks dumbfounded.

My heart skips a beat at his words. I want to say yes in a heartbeat, but I know I can't. Not after what he's put me through. "I'm not sure I want to anymore."

The look of shock on his face is one I wish I could photograph. "Okay, I guess I deserve that. But come on, I saw the look in your eyes when we sang together. You love this."

I feel my resolve slipping. "Fine. I'll think about it." Before he can say another word, I scurry off the stage and head toward Lola. She is still sitting at the same table, only now Ryker inhabits my seat. He is leaning over the table on his elbows, and Lola is inclining her body close to his as they talk.

Lola's head pops up when I approach.

"Whoa, what was that all about?"

I feel my cheeks warming again. "I don't know. It was crazy, right?"

"Not that crazy," Ryker interjects. "You two are great together."

"What are you talking about?" I ask, defens-ively.

Ryker's eyes widen. "Just that your voices blend well together."

My shoulders soften, the tension in them dissipating. I feel like an idiot. Of course he was talking about us being great together musically. Why had I thought he meant something else? Lola purses her lips, giving me a funny look. I can tell she's surprised by my volatile reaction too.

"What was Beckett talking to you about just now?" Lola asks.

"About joining the band." Despite my best efforts, my lips push upward into a smile.

"Cool," Ryker says with a grin. "I'm so glad you're joining us."

"Who said I was?" I cock an eyebrow. "I told him I had to think about it."

"Good for you, girl." Lola holds up her hand exposing her palm, and I give her a high five.

"But you're going to say yes, right?" Ryker looks perplexed.

I shrug. "Maybe."

"Man, Beckett's gonna be pissed." Ryker

stands, running a hand through his hair. "He never apologizes. Ever."

"He still didn't," I explain.

"Oh." Ryker bites his lip. "Well, for what it's worth, I really I hope you consider it. You'd make a great addition."

I nod. "I'll let you know."

Ryker smiles at Lola. "And I'll see you later."

Lola's cheeks turn pink as he saunters off. I nudge her in the shoulder. "What was that about?"

"Nothing."

"That was not nothing. I can see it all over your face."

"Okay." Lola stands up, her face flushed. "I may have given him my phone number, and he may have asked me out, but I'm not one to gossip."

I laugh. "That's great, Lola. You two are cute together."

"Yeah, so are you and Beckett." She elbows me in the side, a teasing gleam in her eye.

Swallowing hard, I scour the room looking for him. When I spot him in the arms of some platinum blond, my stomach tightens. Oh, well. It's not like anything is ever going to happen between us anyway.

4

Beckett

I don't know what possessed me to invite Star up on stage. It's just that when I saw her sitting in the crowd staring up at me with those large innocent eyes I acted without thinking. I felt bad about our last encounter and wanted to make it up to her. Besides, I figured if she's going to be in our band now I should probably make amends.

As she makes her way up to the stage, I take in her outfit. She wears skinny jeans and a tight top, and for the first time I notice how nice her body is. Her sandals tap on the slick stage as she walks tentatively toward me. Her hair is sleek against her face and her lips shine under the bright lights. When her eyes meet mine, I can't help myself. My flirtatious side comes out to play and I motion her forward with a smile and roll of my finger. I see that she notices the lack of keyboard and extra microphone, so I hold mine between us. Surprise is evident on her face, and my heart flips at her open expression. Star hasn't learned to mask her feelings. Every thought is painted all over her face. A part of me is intrigued by this and the other part is completely unnerved.

"The song is called *Can't Have*," I speak to the crowd. Then I lower my gaze and I start playing. As I sing through the verse I'm careful not to make eye contact with Star. But when we reach the chorus and her voice rings out, my eyes lift to hers. Her lips are pressed against the mic between us and I find my gaze lingering on them. Her body moves ever so slightly as she sings, and it's damn sexy. Her lips are pursed and I'm acutely aware of the fact that if I move the microphone out of the way we would totally be making out. I wish I could say that this didn't tempt me in the least, but then I'd be a liar. In fact, through the rest of the song all I can think about is kissing her. Ironic that the lyrics are about wanting something you can't have. Star is someone I need to stay as far away from as possible. She's too good for me. I hardly know her, and yet that's painfully obvious. I won't drag her into all of my garbage. When the song finishes, it takes me a minute to compose myself. I get a little satisfaction out of seeing how dazed Star seems to be too.

Only it's probably more about the rush of singing on stage. I doubt she spent the entire song thinking about kissing me. It's obvious by the dazed look on her face that she's relishing the feeling of performing in front of a crowd. Not that I blame her. There really is nothing like it.

"Thanks for coming," I speak into the mic. "Good night." I unhook my guitar strap while the other guys start cleaning up the stage, and the crowd claps. After setting the guitar down, I turn to Star. "Thanks for singing with me. I know I caught you off guard."

The awed look she held a few minutes ago fades, replaced by a hard look. "Sure."

"Look, I know I was an ass the other night. It's just that Ryker sprung you on me at the last minute, and I wasn't really prepared."

"Well, maybe you'll be prepared for the next girl who auditions."

I almost laugh at her behavior. It's clear that she's trying really hard to make me pay for how I treated her the other night. Only the truth is, that even when she's acting mad she still seems so sweet. And even though I know the best thing to do is to push her away, I really do want her in the band now. "Star," I say, using my best pleading voice. I've never had a girl refuse me when I use this voice. In fact, I kind of feel sorry for her. I know how badly she wants to be upset with me. "All the guys in the band thought you were amazing."

"What about you?" She crosses her arms over her chest, surprising me. "What did you think?"

I squirm, realizing that my charm isn't working as well as I'd hoped. Perhaps I underestimated Star. "I thought you were good."

"Good, huh? That's not what you said the other night."

Man, this chick isn't going to let me off the hook at all. "I just told you that I wasn't in the mood for an audition the other night. I just wanted to jam, okay?" Giggling fills the air and I glance down to see a few girls standing at the edge of the stage staring up at me. I smile back. Now that's what I'm talking about. Clearly they aren't immune to my charm.

"Fan club?" Star asks, unimpressed.

"What can I say? Chicks dig me." *At least most of them do*.

She turns around. "Well, thanks for letting me sing with you. Have fun with your fan club."

I've never been one to beg. I should just let her walk away. But my arm juts out and I grab her wrist before I can stop myself. "Wait, Star. You didn't give me an answer."

She turns slowly. "You didn't ask me a question."

"Oh, I thought I made myself clear. Are you in or not?"

"In what?" She furrows her brows.

"The band."

"I'm not sure I want to anymore."

Seriously? That's unexpected. "Okay, I guess I deserve that. But come on, I saw the look in your eyes when we sang together. You love this."

"Fine. I'll think about it."

When she stomps off the stage, I think about how she really is a lot like Quinn. The thought causes my stomach to clench, and I scold myself for getting involved with Star at all. The platinum blond standing by the stage catches my eye. She's no natural beauty like Star, but she'll definitely be a nice distraction. And that's exactly what I need right now – a distraction. I swagger toward her and lower myself until I'm sitting on the edge of the stage with my legs dangling over the side.

"Hey, beautiful, what's your name?"

The blond leans forward, a smile on her bright pink lips. "Candy."

Perfect. I rest my hand on her arm and move forward until my lips are practically touching her cheek. "What a coincidence. I love candy." I brush my mouth over her ear. "I bet you're just as sweet as candy, aren't you?"

She giggles, her cheeks turning red. The other girls grumble and walk off, while Candy snakes her arm around me. My gaze lands on Star just a few tables away talking to Ryker. When her eyes drift over to me, I see the disgust on her face, and my stomach sinks. Candy's fingers dance up my back, drawing my attention back to her. I glance down at her toned legs and ample cleavage and smile. *This is going to be too easy.*

"Candy, what do you say we get outta here?" I stand up. "Let me just get my stuff together. Wait for me, okay?"

"Of course." She grins, leaning against the stage while I head toward my guitar. I force myself not to look at Star, but for some reason I can't seem to keep my thoughts off of her. I've never had this issue before. I don't obsess about girls. Hell, I won't ever think about Candy again after tonight. This is my pattern. I hook up with girls after a show and move on. So, why is Star getting under my skin like this? I glance back at her. It must just be her resemblance to Quinn. Yes, that's it. She's just bringing up too many emotions and memories for me, that's all. But she's not Quinn. I have to remember that.

5
Star

"How was your date with Ryker?" I turn around in my chair and abandon the homework I've been working on for hours. My fingers are kinked and sore, so I wriggle them out. A strand of hair slips out of my loose ponytail and I push it out of my face, tucking it behind my ear.

"It was fun." Lola drops her purse on her bed and perches on the edge. Even though she keeps her face neutral, I can see that she is suppressing a grin.

"That good, huh?" I rest my chin on the back of the chair.

"Yeah, it was, actually. Ryker is a lot of fun." She slips off her heels and pushes them aside with her toe. Then she peers up at me with a serious look that I know too well.

"Uh-oh," I say. "What's up?"

"It's just that Ryker kept asking me if you're going to join the band." She fidgets with the bottom of her skirt. "Have you decided what you're going to do?"

"I'm not sure." I bite my lip.

"Look, Star, I saw you on stage. You were in your element, and I could tell you loved every minute of it. So, what's up?"

I think of how Beckett tossed me aside after my first audition, and how he was all over that blond chick at the club. Then I remember how I felt when we sang together, and my stomach tightens. "I just can't stand how hot and cold Beckett is. It's not something I want to put up with."

"Man, this guy really gets under your skin," Lola observes with a grin.

"Yeah, he does," I admit. Let's face it, I can't keep anything from Lola anyway. "That's why I don't think I can join the band."

Lola's lips curl downward. "Ryker's gonna be disappointed."

"What's his deal, anyway? Why does he care so much?"

Lola shrugs. "He just wants what's best for the band, and he thinks that's you."

I can tell by the look on her face there is more to the story, but I don't press. It doesn't matter. I'm not joining Beckett, and that's the end of the story.

"When are you going to tell Beckett?"

"I'm not. Ryker gave me his number that

first night we met. I'll call him and he can relay the news to Beckett." I give Lola a pouty look. "Unless you want to tell him for me?"

"No way." She throws up her arms in surrender. "And have him shoot the messenger? I don't think so."

"Fair enough." I giggle. "I'll call him tomorrow."

It's a little after nine in the morning when I dial the number Ryker gave me. My fingers tremble, causing the slip of paper in my hand to shake. It rings numerous times before a groggy voice mumbles an almost unintelligible greeting. I feel bad for calling so early. It's just that I want to get the whole thing over with. I don't want to think about this all day during classes.

"Ryker, it's Star. I'm sorry for calling so early."

Laughing fills the line, causing me to stiffen. "This isn't Ryker."

"It's not?"

"Believe me, it's not." The amused tone causes my insides to coil.

"I'm sorry. I must have the wrong number." My gaze connects with the paper between my fingers, and I wonder if I dialed incorrectly.

"It's Beckett."

The words stop me cold. I swallow hard, working to find my voice. "Oh, I didn't know. Ryker gave me this number, and I just assumed it was his."

"Yes, you would think so, wouldn't you?" He responds dryly. "I'll have to talk to Ryker about him handing out my number without asking."

Anger sparks. "Don't worry. I don't plan to use it again."

"It's fine." His voice is gentle, and it surprises me. "I don't mind you having it. I just want to make sure he doesn't give it to anyone else. Besides, as a member of my band you should have my number."

I bite my lip. "About that—"

"That's why you called, right?" he cuts me off. "To let me know you decided to join Beckett?"

I'm astounded at this guy's confidence. What makes him so sure I'm going to say yes to his offer? He must not be used to people turning him down. I smile, thinking how I'll relish being the first.

"I'm actually glad you called," he says. "I was up all night writing a new song, and I really think the two of us will sound great on it. We'll work on it tonight, okay?"

"Tonight?"

"Yeah, for band practice. You're coming, aren't you?"

I know I should say no. That was the plan, after all. But the thought of Beckett writing a song late into the night with the intention of us singing it together throws my whole plan out of whack. I clear my throat. "Of course."

"Great. See you at seven," he responds. It's odd, but I can actually hear the smile in his voice. It causes my heart to soar.

"Okay." I intentionally keep my tone calm, hoping he doesn't sense how elated I am.

"And Star?"

"Yes?" I hold my breath.

"Don't ever call me before noon again."

"Right." I click off, irritated. How does he do that? How can he make me so happy one minute and so infuriated the next? I throw my cell down on my bed and groan. Did I seriously just agree to join Beckett? Man, that guy really knows how to push my buttons. Lola's going to have a field day with this one.

The door to our dorm room pops open and Lola rushes in, two paper coffee cups in hand. Her hair is a little disheveled, and pink flushes her cheeks. She's wearing a cute belted black sweater over skinny jeans and black boots.

"I figured you could use a little pick me up this morning." She shoves a cup into my hand.

The one that only moments ago was holding my cell phone. I wrap my fingers around the warmth of it and take a sip. Chocolaty creaminess swims down my throat. "Hmm. Thanks, Lola."

"Sure." She runs a hand down her hair, and the glossy black strands are sleek again.

I touch the long strands of my brown hair wishing they were as shiny and sleek as Lola's. Sure my hair is straight and thick, but it's unruly and has a total mind of its own.

"So, are you going to keep me in suspense all day? Tell me what happened when you called Ryker."

My face goes hot. "Um…well, I didn't exactly call Ryker."

Lola pulls the cup away from her dark red lips. "You chickened out, huh?"

"Not exactly." My stomach churns.

Lola knits her brows together. "What do you mean?"

"Ryker didn't give me his number. He gave me Beckett's."

"Ah." Lola raises a knowing eyebrow. "So how did he take it?"

I stall by taking a large gulp of the coffee. After swallowing I say, "Really well, actually."

"Jerk," Lola mutters under her breath.

I giggle. "There was nothing to be upset about, since I sort of told him I'd join the band."

"No way!" Lola almost spills her coffee. "What made you change your mind?"

I shrug my shoulders. "I don't know. I was all set to tell him, but then he started talking about a song he wrote for us and I just couldn't do it."

"Ooh, he wrote a song for you." Lola perches on the edge of her bed, her coffee cup still in her hand. "Do tell."

"Not for me, exactly. He just said that he thought we would sound great on it."

"Star Evans, it sounds like maybe Mr. Rockstar has a little crush on you."

I bat away her words. "Please, he so doesn't."

Lola smirks. "If you say so."

My stomach flutters from her words. I know I shouldn't want them to be true. Beckett's all wrong for me. Besides, he's an arrogant jerk. I'm usually super practical, and I always go for the good guys. Why is it that I can't seem to temper the attraction I feel for Beckett?

I slide into a seat at the very back of the large lecture hall just as my history class starts. Professor Johnston doesn't waste any time, but immediately starts his lecture. I fumble around in my backpack, my fingers brushing over my notebooks and papers. Grasping my history notebook, I yank it out. I quietly unzip the front pocket and reach inside to protract a pen while the professor drones on. Just as I sit upright and open my notebook, the dark haired girl to my left bends toward me. "You're her, aren't you?" she whispers. "The girl with Beckett?"

I'm startled by the question, thinking how I just decided to join less than an hour ago. Does news really travel that fast? "Um…yeah, I guess. I mean, I'm in the band if that's what you're asking."

"I'm Stacy." She says with a smile.

"Star," I respond, leaning closer to the girl, but keeping my eyes fixed at the front of the room to make sure we're not caught by Professor Johnston. "How did you know that I was in the band?"

"Oh, I was at the bar the other night when you two sang together." The girl clutches her chest, a dreamy look cloaking her face. "You're so lucky. I would give anything to have Beckett sing to me like he did to you."

My cheeks warm. "He wasn't singing to me. We're not…um…we're not together really. I'm just the backup singer."

"Still. It's every girl's dream in this town. Beckett is like one of the biggest local bands here in Seattle."

"Really?"

"Oh, yeah. They play everywhere." Stacy smiles. "But why am I the one telling you this? You're in the band, right?"

"Right." I squirm uncomfortably in my chair as her words hit me like a ton of bricks. I knew Beckett was good, but I didn't realize they were also well known. A part of me is excited by the prospect, but the other part of me is sickened. What have I gotten myself into?

6
Beckett

I should be mad at Ryker for giving out my phone number, but I'm not. It was actually nice to answer the phone and hear Star's voice on the other end, even if it was way too early in the morning. I stumble into the dirty kitchen and fumble around for the coffee maker. I fill the pitcher with water and then scoop some coffee grounds into the filter. Then I push it on and lean against the sticky counter, running a hand over my head. Footsteps pound down the hallway, causing my pulse to spike. Who's here?

I push myself off the counter, the hair on the back of my neck prickling. I reach across the counter for the set of knives, and fish out the largest one. Then I inch forward quietly. When a shadow casts on the carpet, I jump forward.

"Shit, man. Are you gonna stab me?"

Startled, I drop the knife. It clatters to the floor, landing mere inches from my bare feet. "Tate, what are you doing here?"

"I live here, bro." Tate pushes past me, his long hair brushing over his shoulders.

"Since when?" I lean over, retrieving the knife before one of us steps on it. "I haven't seen you for months."

"I was working out of town." Tate opens a cupboard and pulls out a coffee mug. His flannel pants hang low on his hips, a tattered wife beater tank top hanging over it.

"You better not have brought any drugs into our apartment." I toss the knife back on the counter.

"I'm clean, man."

"I hope so," I mumble.

Tate turns around to face me. "You know I haven't used since…"

I shake my head, not wishing him to say it. We both know the event he's referencing, and neither of us wants to rehash it. "Yeah, I know."

"So I hear you've got some hot chick in your band now." Tate smiles while pouring a cup of coffee.

"Who told you that?" My stomach knots. The last person I want Star to meet is my brother.

"Mom told me."

"You talked to Mom? When?"

"Last night. She told me all about what's been going on with you."

"Surprised she even knows," I say pushing

past Tate to get my own coffee.

"Lighten up on her, dude. She just wants a better life for you, you know."

"Yes, I know she and dad want me to quit music and do something more stable. Too bad for them, it's my life." Reaching into the cupboard, I pull down a mug. "It's not like I'm going to make the same mistakes you guys did."

"No, I'm pretty sure you'll make different ones." Tate laughs in that condescending older brother tone.

I just roll my eyes and take a sip of my drink. The last person I need to take advice from is Tate. He's one of the main reasons I live my life the way I do. I try to do the exact opposite of him.

"So tell me about this hot chick. You doing her yet?"

For some reason this angers me. "No, I'm not."

"Whoa! How long has she been a part of the band?"

"Just since this morning, actually, but she auditioned a couple of weeks ago. Then she and I sang together the other night."

"And you still haven't slept with her? That must be some kind of record for you, huh?" Tate nudges me in the side. "So, I'm guessing she's not hot then."

"Oh, no, believe me, she's hot."

55

"Is there something you want to tell me, bro?" Tate scrunches up his forehead. "You're still into chicks, right?"

I sigh, frustrated. "What exactly did Mom tell you? I didn't even know she knew about Star. And I know she didn't say she was hot."

"No, she just said that Ryker mentioned her," Tate explains, and now it all makes sense.

"Yeah, I bet he did."

"Oh, I see. So she's doing Ryker." Tate slaps me on the back. "I'm proud of you, dude. You finally adhere to the guy code."

I shrug him off. "I'm not adhering to any code. Ryker isn't doing her. I think he's into her friend."

"Then what's going on?"

"Nothing. She's just a girl in our band, end of story." I head toward my room, coffee mug still in hand. Warmth seeps into my fingers. "I've got a lot to do today, so we'll have to talk later." I pause. "Are you going to be around awhile this time?"

Tate nods. "Yeah, I am."

"Cool." Even though I was irritated when I first saw him this morning, I have to admit that I'm glad he's back. When he took off I was kind of worried. Tate and I may have our issues, but I don't want to lose him. I know exactly how it feels to lose someone you love, and I never want to experience it again.

7
Star

I'm late like always. I pull up to Beckett's house ten minutes after seven, my heart beating erratically in my chest. Despite how hard I tried to be on time, I just couldn't get it together. *Story of my life.* After cutting the engine, I yank my purse off the passenger seat and jump out of the car. The garage door is already open, so I walk toward it pushing a few loose strands of hair from my face. Ryker stands clustered with the other two guys in the band, while Beckett fiddles with one of the amps. The minute I step inside, Ryker glances up at me with a smile.

"You made it." He motions me over. As I move toward him I glance over at Beckett, but he is still busy with his task. I try not to feel disappointed that Ryker seems to be more excited about my presence than Beckett. "Star, this is Jimmy, our drummer."

I smile at the tall, lanky guy with long dark hair, and he grins back.

"And this is Pierce, our electric guitar player."

"You were awesome the other night." Pierce smiles, his floppy hair bouncing around his face, reminding me of a puppy with long ears.

"Thanks." I'm grateful for the compliment, and start to relax a little.

"Are we gonna stand around yapping like a bunch of girls all night or get to work?" Beckett barks, and my shoulders stiffen.

Ryker gives me an apologetic look while the other guys grumble. I press my lips together and turn around, annoyed with Beckett for his grumpy attitude. Would it really kill the guy to be friendly every once in awhile? From my few encounters with him I can tell that his social skills are seriously lacking. The other guys scramble to their instruments, and the garage rumbles as the amps roar to life. As I head toward the keyboard, I make the mistake of peering over at Beckett. His head is bent down as he slips his guitar strap on. Today he wears a short sleeved shirt, exposing the intricate tattoos weaving his upper arm. As if he senses me staring, he lifts his head. I freeze, just as a slow smile spreads across his face.

"See something you like?" He drawls.

"No," I sputter, my face turning so hot I fear I'll melt my makeup. "Why?"

"I thought you were noticing my new

guitar. It's pretty slick, huh?" He smirks. "What did you think I meant?"

"Nothing." I take a deep breath, and lower myself down onto the bench in front of the keyboard. *What the hell is wrong with me? I need to hold it together around this guy if I plan to be in this band very long.*

"Okay, guys." Beckett grins at me. "And girl. I have a new song I want us to try. If we can get the hang of it maybe we can add it to the roster for Saturday night's gig. If not, we'll hold off for now."

"Saturday night?" I ask meekly.

Beckett nods, tossing a couple of papers in my direction. "Yeah, we're playing at the pub."

I catch the sheets of paper before they flutter to the ground. "What pub?"

"Don't worry," Beckett says, turning back around and strumming once on his guitar. "We'll talk details later. Right now, it's time to play."

I face forward, my eyes connecting with the papers in front of me. This must be the new song Beckett wrote. A tiny wave of excitement pulses through me as I touch the keys, and the rest of the band swells behind me. The beat of the drums pulsate beneath my feet, causing my whole body to buzz. Beckett starts to sing in his husky voice, and chills brush over my skin. Just like everything I've heard the band play, the song has a haunting melody, the lyrics dark. I decide to try out the harmony on the chorus. Pressing my lips to the mic above the keyboard, I sing with Beckett.

I'm untouchable
Just out of reach
And I'm not able
To break free
It's who I am
It's me

Glancing over at Beckett, I wonder about his tortured lyrics. He always acts as if he doesn't have a care in the world, but nobody writes songs like his if they haven't endured some kind of pain or neglect. Lifting my head a little, I stare at his face while he sings the next verse. His eyes are cast downward, his hands moving slowly and methodically over the guitar. Only I can tell that in his mind he is a million miles away. I find myself hoping that one day he'll share his feelings with me. For some reason his need to be so mysterious and distant, only draws me to him more. When I hear the verse coming to a close, I force my head away from him and get ready to sing the chorus with him again.

When the practice ends, I gather up my sheet music and get ready to head home. The rush I feel from the last couple of hours hasn't died down yet and it's like I'm floating above the ground as I make my way around the keyboard. I approach Beckett who is bent over his guitar.

"So, about that gig on Saturday night?" I ask, while my shadow casts over his shoulder.

He peers up at me, his eyebrow raising. "Yeah, I'll pick you up around six, okay?"

This catches me off guard, and I freeze. After swallowing hard, I find my voice, "Okay."

"You live in the dorms, right?" He sets down his guitar, and stands to face me.

My heart beats frantically in my chest, and my palms fill with moisture. Since I can't speak with him looking at me the way he is I just nod.

"My apartment is pretty close to the campus." He runs a hand over his head. "So it makes sense just to swing by on my way to the pub. I'll meet you in the parking lot."

I nod again, wishing my mouth would move, but it's like my lips are glued together all of the sudden.

He smirks at my lack of response. "See ya then, Star."

"Yeah," I finally squeak out, and start to turn around.

"Oh, and Star?"

I whirl around to face him.

"Wear a little skirt or something on Saturday." He grins.

My face heats up. "Excuse me?"

"Well, we already give the girls plenty of

eye candy at our shows." He gives me a knowing look that irritates me. "Why not offer something to the guys?"

I roll my eyes. Did he seriously just say that? "You're a pig."

"So is that a yes or no then on the skirt?" He looks confused.

I groan in frustration, and then I turn around to face the other band members. "Bye, guys. See you Saturday."

They all wave in response.

"Hey, do you need a ride on Saturday?" Ryker asks, stepping toward me.

"No, I've got it, man," Beckett speaks from over my shoulder.

Ryker lifts his brows a little. My head is swirling from all the mixed signals. Before anyone can say anything else to me, I race out of the garage clutching the sheet music to my chest. When I reach my car, I take a deep breath. I swear every time I'm with Beckett I feel like I've endured whiplash. One minute I'm swooning over him, the next I want to gouge his eyes out with a dull spoon. He's so infuriating.

Despite my frustration at Beckett's request, I actually do wear a skirt on Saturday night. It's short too, and tight. I have no idea what possesses me to put it on. Once I catch my reflection in the mirror Lola and I have mounted to the door, I feel mortified. I won't even be able to move on the stage without giving every guy in the audience a sneak peek. I'm about to take it off when Lola marches in.

"Wow, what are you wearing?"

My cheeks flush. "Nothing. I was just about to change." I fiddle with the bottom of the skirt.

"Why? You look hot. Like a sexy rocker chick." Lola runs a finger through her hair.

I move back over to the mirror and assess myself. The large silver hoop earrings peek out from underneath my straight brown hair, my eyes are lined in dark black eyeliner and shimmer shadow, and my lips are lightly glossed. Several bangle bracelets line my arm. I have on a white floaty top over my skirt, and my feet are encased in strappy sandals. I try to imagine Beckett's reaction when he sees me in this, and it causes my heart to flip in my chest. He's only ever seen me in jeans before. Glancing at the clock, I cringe. It's already six. Beckett is probably already waiting outside.

"Okay." I sigh. "I guess this is it then."

"Ooh, this is so exciting," Lola squeals. "Have fun. I'll be there later to hear you perform."

I nod, pressing my shiny lips together. Then I grab my purse and head out to meet Beckett.

Once my feet hit the parking lot pavement, I realize I don't know what kind of car Beckett drives. I scour the lot and find a truck idling, its headlights painting the ground in front. Tentatively I head toward it. When I get close enough I can see Beckett sitting in the driver's side, his arm slung out the window. I keep walking forward, even though I'm feeling incredibly nervous, especially when I glance down at my half naked body. With trembling fingers I open the passenger door and slip inside. The scent of vinyl seats, the crisp night air and Beckett's spicy cologne fills my senses. Rock music plays faintly through the speakers.

"So, you took my advice, huh?" Beckett reaches out, his fingers skimming my skirt. It causes goosebumps to rise on my legs, and I suppress a shiver.

He's wearing a white t-shirt, and tight jeans, and it takes all my willpower to avert my gaze. I shrug my shoulders. "I guess I did."

"You're really gonna mess up our image, you know?"

My head whips in his direction, fearing that he's just shot me down again. "What do you mean?"

"Well, we've always had a predominately female audience. I'm thinking after tonight we're going to have a lot of male fans." His gaze roves over every inch of my body.

I have to work hard to slow down the racing of my heart. "Isn't that you wanted?"

He bites down on his lip. "I'm not sure." After giving me a contemplative look, he puts his car in drive and heads out of the parking lot. I'm grateful that he's shifted his intense gaze away from me. Now I can breathe normally. I stare out the window at the dark night sky as we head down the street.

"What are you studying in school?" Beckett asks, startling me.

I shrug. "I'm a business major. Not quite sure what I want to do yet."

"You don't want to study the stars like your dad, huh?"

I giggle, tucking an errant piece of hair behind my ear. "No. I've had enough star gazing to last a lifetime."

Beckett chuckles. "Star gazing. That's funny."

I furrow my brows, and then realize that he must think I made a pun about my name. Deciding to just go with it, I let out a light laugh. Glancing over at him, I ask, "What about you? Are you in college?"

He shakes his head while keeping his eyes trained on the road in front of him. "No. I've always known I want to be a musician, so after high school I just decided to pursue that. Didn't exactly thrill my parents, but it's my life, you know?"

"Yeah." I think about how I haven't even told my parents I'm in this band. They wouldn't be too happy about it. They want me to focus on school and nothing else while I'm here. And since they're paying for it, I figure the less they know about my extracurricular activities the better. Peering over at Beckett, I wonder how old he is. He looks older than me, but I can't be sure. Then again, that's not exactly a question I'm comfortable asking him.

"So," Beckett's voice breaks into the silence, "that first night you auditioned for us, was that an original piece you played?"

"Yeah," I respond.

"You like to write songs?"

"I love it, but I don't do it as often as I like," I answer truthfully.

"Okay, well, let's plan on doing it tomorrow night."

Shocked, I furrow my brow. "Do what?"

"Write songs," Beckett says in his normal bored tone, keeping his eyes trained on the road. "None of the other guys in the band write, and we need some new material, so I figured you and I could come up with some new stuff. We can meet at my apartment. I'll give you the address later."

I wonder if Beckett will ever cease to amaze me. He's the only guy I've ever met that I can't get a read on at all. Maybe after I've spent some more time with him he'll become less of a mystery. I smile to myself, thinking about how much I'm looking forward to spending some alone time with him tomorrow night.

8
Beckett

I can't believe she actually wore the skirt. I was kind of just teasing her when I asked her to wear it. Now I'm not sure that was a good idea. The eyes of every guy in the place are glued to Star's legs, including mine. And that's not a good thing. I need to keep my distance from Star, not lust after her. For some reason this girl makes me act differently, and I'm not sure I like it. I mean, why did I invite her over to write with me? I hate writing with other people. I'm not exactly the collaborative type. But when she sat in my car smelling like honeysuckle and looking all sexy, I couldn't help it. The thought of getting her alone got me so excited.

It would have just been easier to hit on her after the show and take her back to my place. But that's not how I want things to go between Star and me. No, she's a part of our band, and I have to respect her. I can't treat her like just another hookup.

"Ready?" Ryker interrupts my thoughts.

I nod, forcing myself out of my reverie. "Yeah."

"You okay, man? You seem out of it." Ryker furrows his brows.

"I'm fine." I shrug, hoping he'll just let it go. Only Ryker knows me too well. "It's just that Tate's back." I'm hoping this response will appease him and he won't find out that I can't stop thinking about the girl he brought into our band.

"Oh." Ryker nods, a look of understanding on his face. "Is he…you know?"

"Clean?" I finish. "Yeah, I think so. It just changes the dynamics for me at home, you know?"

"Give it up for Beckett," A male voice booms through the microphone.

"That's our cue." Pierce slaps me on the back as he brushes past.

Ryker gives me a concerned look. "You gonna be okay?"

"Hey, you know me. I'm always fine." I smile at him as Jimmy passes us and makes his way up the steps. Ryker turns from me to follow him. I'm just about to climb the stairs myself when Star appears next to me. She's breathing funny and her hands are shaking.

I lean close to her, and lightly tap her arm. "You okay?"

She nods, her face reddening.

"Hey. You're gonna be fine," I assure her.

"Okay." She forces a smile and takes a tentative step forward. Without meaning to, my gaze lands on her butt as she makes her way up to the stage. Man, I really need to stop checking her out. I shake my head and walk swiftly over to my guitar. After strapping it on, I step toward the microphone. The drums kick up behind me, and I reach down to strum my guitar. As the song plays, I glance over at Star. She still looks terrified, but I can tell she's working hard to mask it. I feel kind of bad for the girl. Clearly this is all new to her. While I sing out the first verse, I keep my eyes trained on her. Finally she peers up at me, our eyes locking. I give her an encouraging smile and nod as we near the chorus. She grins and presses her mouth to the microphone. As soon as her voice rings out I know she'll be fine.

After a couple more songs, Star totally opens up. She's swaying her hips back and forth, and I find myself mesmerized. I shake my head and keep my mouth up against the microphone so I don't miss my cue. Through the remainder of the set I try not to look at Star. I need to stay focused on the music.

"What a rush," Star says the minute our

final set is over. Her face is flushed, her eyes bright. She runs a hand through her hair and walks toward me. "Do you ever get used to it?"

I grin. "It never gets old, if that's what you're asking." Clattering sounds behind us as the guys put away their equipment.

Star glances around. "Do you need help with anything?"

I want to tell her yes to keep her up here with me, but I look down and see the girl she's always with sitting at a table near the stage. "Nah, it's okay. Go hang out with your friend. You're done for the night."

She looks a little disappointed, which surprises me. I assumed she wanted an out. "Aren't you taking me home?" The vulnerable expression on her face causes my stomach to twist.

"Can't your friend take you? Ryker said she's your roommate."

Her face falls. "Um…yeah, I'm sure she can." Star fidgets with her bracelets. "I just thought…well, never mind."

"What?" I stop her. "What did you think?"

She shakes her head. "Nothing. It's fine. We still on for tomorrow?"

I know I should say no, but it kills me to see the disappointment in her eyes. I don't want to do that again. "Yeah. I'll text you my address."

She bites her lip, and it's so damn cute I have to look away. When she leaves the stage, Ryker approaches me. "You giving Star a ride home?"

"Nah, she's going with her friend."

"Oh." Ryker narrows his eyes. "I was kind of hoping for a little alone time with Lola, but that's cool."

My gaze lingers on Star as she heads over to her friend. I'm looking forward to tomorrow night a little too much, and it makes me wonder what the hell I'm doing.

My chest tightens when I notice the time. Star will be here any minute and the place is a disaster. It's pretty obvious that this is a bachelor pad. I snatch a couple of empty soda cans off the coffee table. When I race into the kitchen to throw them away, I bump into Tate.

"Whoa, what's going on out here?" He cocks his eyebrow like he's impressed. "You cleaning?"

"Just picking up. Star's coming over to write lyrics with me."

"You invited the new girl in your band over here to write with you?" His eyes widen.

"Yes." I sigh exasperated.

"Are you serious? Wow, I've got to meet

this girl."

I straighten the rock n' roll magazines on the end table. "It's not that big of a deal."

"Oh, I beg to differ, bro. You hate writing with other people and you've never invited a girl up here for any activity that doesn't take place inside your bedroom."

"That's not true," I scoff.

"It isn't? Name one then?"

I rack my brain for a second and then realize that he's right. Shame fills me.

"See? What did I say?" Tate grins. "This girl must be something."

"It's not like that, Tate. She's just a girl in my band. We're working on songs. That's it."

"Sure." He nods slowly, that stupid grin still on his face.

A knock on the door interrupts us, and my heart stops.

"You gonna answer that, bro?" Tate flashes me a bemused smile.

I point at Tate. "Look, Star isn't like the girls I normally bring around, so be on your best behavior."

"Man, you really like this chick."

I glare at him. "And don't say things like that."

He throws his hands up in surrender. "Okay, okay. I won't say anything stupid. Now answer the door."

I swing it open. Star stands in the hallway, a notebook pressed to her chest. She's wearing jeans and a t-shirt, and her hair is pulled back in a messy bun. A few strands have already fallen out of it, and I imagine yanking the rest of it out as well. I swallow hard and wonder once again why I invited her here.

"Hey," she says in her soft voice.

I nod and step aside. "Come in."

She brushes past me, her sweet scent washing over me.

After closing the door I say, "Star, this is my brother Tate. He lives here."

"Nice to meet you." She thrusts out her hand, and he shakes it.

"Tate was actually just leaving," I add.

"But I can stay if you need some help with your songwriting." Tate smirks at me.

"Oh, are you a musician too?" Star asks in her kind, innocent way.

"No, he's not." I give him a sharp look.

"What Beckett means is that I'm no longer in a band," Tate clarifies. "But yes, I am a musician."

I clamp my hand on his shoulder. "Well, you better get going to that thing you have tonight."

"Ah, yes, wouldn't want to be late for that

thing." Tate says sarcastically, and I want to kick him in the shin. Star looks on with amusement as Tate heads out the door. I exhale once he's gone.

"I didn't know you lived with your brother," Star says.

"Yeah, well, he's in the construction business and he works all over. So, he's not always around."

"You two seem close."

I rub the back of my neck. I don't usually talk this much to girls about my life and it's making me nervous. "Yeah, I guess. Anyway, you want something to drink or eat or anything?" I feel like an idiot, but I honestly have no idea how to behave. This is literally the first time I've had to play host to someone.

"No, I'm okay."

"So." I tap the notebook still pressed to her chest. "Is that your songwriting book?"

"Yeah, it is." She smiles.

"Then let's get to it."

9
Star

After scrawling the words on the paper, I look up at Beckett while chewing on the end of my pen. "Okay, what about this? You're my sunny sky, the gentle breeze, making me weak in the knees."

Beckett raises a brow, the side of his mouth curling upward. "Seriously?"

My stomach clenches. I release my notebook and it falls into my lap. "What?"

"It's just that songwriting is about reaching deep inside of yourself and exposing your raw feelings. These lyrics are shallow. It's like you're afraid to do more than scratch the surface."

"Well, I'm sorry that my songs aren't all sad and depressing like yours, but that doesn't mean my lyrics are shallow. I happen to be an upbeat person. These are my feelings."

"Really?" Beckett leans forward, a small smile on his lips. He's so close his breath feathers over my skin. "Then tell me who makes you weak in the knees."

I swallow hard to slow the beating of my heart and sit back. "No one."

"But you said those were your raw feelings. Were you lying to me?"

"No, I mean...well..." I sputter, feeling stupid. "I mean, it's what I want, I guess."

"You want someone to make you weak in the knees." Beckett smirks. "Interesting."

I take a deep breath, willing my heart to slow down. Reaching down, I flip to a clean page in my notebook. "Okay, so you don't like those lyrics. I'll write something different."

Beckett stands up. "What about the song you sang when I first met you?"

I look up from the blank page. "But you already know it. I thought you wanted something new and fresh."

"I do." Beckett walks toward his kitchen. I try not to openly gawk at his backside. "I was just wondering who you wrote that song for."

"Oh." I swallow back the disgust, thinking of Spencer. "I wrote that for my ex-boyfriend."

After reaching in his fridge and pulling out a couple of bottled waters, Beckett turns to me. "And did you write a song about him after you broke up?"

I shake my head.

"Why not?" He swaggers back into the room.

"There was no reason to. I didn't want to think about him anymore at all." Honestly, I was so hurt over our breakup that I could barely crawl out of bed for weeks, let alone write a song about it.

Beckett drops the bottled waters on the coffee table, his eyes alight with excitement. "See, that's what I'm talking about. You're afraid of your own feelings."

Anger ignites in my gut. "Oh, you're one to talk."

"What's that supposed to mean?" His eyes darken, and it should scare me. Only it doesn't. For some reason it just makes him look more sexy. God, I hate how everything he does attracts me.

"I just can't believe you're talking about me being afraid of my feelings. Look at you." I point at him with my index finger. "All of your songs are about keeping people at a distance. You shut everyone out."

"That's not true."

"Name one person you're close to."

Beckett scoots forward until our knees our touching. "You." He speaks so softly I barely hear him.

I freeze. "Me?"

"Yeah." His teasing smile is back. "Look at how close we are. You're practically in my lap."

Annoyed, I move away until my back hits

the armrest. "C'mon, Beckett, you know that's not what I mean."

"Fine." He throws his arms up in surrender. "Maybe you're right. Maybe I have some fatal flaw and I don't know how to be close to people." He looks me in the eye. "So why don't you teach me?"

"Excuse me?" I cock my head to the side.

"Teach me how to get close to you, Star." His tone is seductive and causes my pulse to race.

"What?" My voice comes out in a high pitched strain, and I mentally slap myself.

"Yeah, you let me teach you to become a better songwriter and you can teach me how to be closer to people."

It's the weirdest thing I've ever heard, but once my eyes lock with Beckett's I know I won't turn down his request. I would say yes to almost anything when he looks at me like that. "Okay, it's a deal."

"Should we shake on it?" He extends his hand and I take it in mine, wishing my palms weren't so sweaty. "So, what's the first lesson?"

"Huh?"

"In getting close to people? What's the first thing I should do?"

I can think of a million things I want him to do to get close to me, but I force my thoughts to a PG level. "First, you can tell me a little about yourself." My eyes scan the room and catch on several posters hanging on the wall. I stand up and walk toward them. "Like, why do you have all these posters of Killjoy? They broke up years ago. Are they like your favorite band or something?"

"Yeah." He says from over my shoulder.

"Really? Why?"

"Because that's my dad." He points to the man in the center of the picture.

My mouth gapes open. I wonder why I never made the connection before. Now that he's staring me in the face, I can see that the resemblance is uncanny. "Barry Nash is your dad?"

Beckett nods.

"Wow, that must've been so cool to have a rockstar for a dad." I smile.

"He wasn't a rockstar by the time I was born." He shrugs. "The band had already broken up."

"Why did they break up?"

Beckett shakes his head. "I think that's enough of a lesson for today, Star." He flashes me a wicked grin. "Now it's my turn to teach you how to write a decent song."

"Decent song?" I raise my eyebrow. "Or tortured, sadistic song?"

"What's the difference?"

I roll my eyes. "You're impossible." While

I follow him back to the couch, I wonder why he evaded my question about his dad. What is the reason Killjoy broke up? I hope that someday Beckett trusts me enough to tell me. After plopping down on the couch, I scoop up my notebook and pen, and tuck my legs under my body. Beckett stretches out on the other side of the couch, staring up at the ceiling. His eyes appear to be closed, and I wonder if he fell asleep.

"Am I interrupting nap time or something?" I ask.

He brings his head back down, opens his eyes and gives me one of those teasing smiles that causes my stomach to flip. "I was thinking. Songwriting takes concentration and quiet. It's not just about slapping some words on a page."

I swallow hard, biting back a defensive remark. "Okay, so what were you just thinking?"

He reaches his hand out, and for one second I think he's going to touch my knee. My heart stops, but then he says, "Hand me my guitar."

I glance to my right and see his guitar propped against the wall. After grabbing it, I hand it to him. He rests it in his lap and strums a haunting chord. Then he opens his mouth and sings,

Pretty smile, innocent eyes,
Open and honest, not a disguise.
Scarred and bruised, innocence stolen,

Ripped away, my heart is broken.

When he stops singing, I realize that I'm holding my breath. I swallow hard. "You just wrote that?"

He nods, his eyes dark. "Writing is therapeutic for me."

"Who is it about?"

Beckett shakes his head. "It's not your turn anymore, Miss Psychiatrist. I'm supposed to be teaching you about writing a song. We already had your lesson."

I have a feeling I can learn more about him by listening to his songs anyway, so I nod. "Fine. But I don't see how you can teach me to write like that."

Beckett sets down his guitar and scoots a little closer to me. "Why not? Haven't you ever experienced anything painful in your life?"

I bite my lip, his proximity causing my heart to race. "Of course."

"Close your eyes."

I do as I'm told.

"Remember an incident that caused you pain. How did you feel about it? What words would you use to describe it?"

He's so close I can feel his breath against my skin and I shiver. I rack my brain for something, anything. But all I can think about is Beckett and how much I want him. So I end up blurting out the first thing that comes to mind. "Desperate."

"Desperate, huh? Okay, we can work with that."

Hearing his teasing tone, I open my eyes. Beckett is staring at me with those dark eyes, and I feel uncomfortable. It's like he can see right through me. "What are you desperate for?"

Feeling like an idiot, I shake my head. "I don't know. Desperate probably wasn't the right word."

"Star." His hand clamps down over mine, and I freeze. The feel of his skin against mine causes a flush of desire to run through me. It's unlike any feeling I've had before. I never felt like this around Spencer or any other boys for that matter. "You're doing great. Now keep going. What are you feeling right now?"

"Desire," I blurt out the word before I can register what I'm saying. Afterward, I clamp my mouth shut. *How lame am I?*

But Beckett doesn't laugh at me. His expression becomes serious. He lifts his arm and tucks a strand of hair behind my ear with his hand. My heart speeds up, and my eyes fall to his lips which are only inches from mine. I want to kiss him more than I've ever wanted to kiss anyone in my life. His eyes sear into mine, and it appears that he wants to kiss me too. He moves forward a little, and I inhale sharply. Then he abruptly sits back, his eyes widening as if he's coming out of a trance. After clearing his throat, he says, "I think that's good for tonight, Star."

It's like he just threw cold water on me. "But we didn't really write anything together."

"We will. Don't worry." He stands up, and I know I'm being dismissed.

I want to ask him what I did wrong, but I don't want to sound like a whiny child. So, I hold my head up high and smile. "This was fun. Thank you."

As I walk past him, his hand lightly brushes my shoulder. "It *was* fun. I look forward to more lessons." He throws me a wink that makes my knees soften.

Composing myself, I nod and hurry out the door. Once I'm safely in the hallway, I lean against the wall and take deep steadying breaths to calm my frantic heartbeat.

10
Beckett

The minute Star leaves, I bang my head against the wall. What the hell just happened? Did she really say she desired me? And was I about to kiss her? I groan and run my hand over my head. I so underestimated that girl. She is seriously dangerous. I need to stay as far away from her as possible.

My cell phone buzzes in my pocket, startling me. I push myself away from the wall and snatch it out of my pocket. *Ryker.*

"Hey, dude, what's up?"

"I just left Lola's. Star there?"

"Not anymore." With the phone pressed to my ear, I make my way to the couch and sink into it. "She just left."

"Please tell me you didn't sleep with her."

"Of course not. We just worked on some songs, that's all." I sigh. "Why do you care anyway? I thought you were into her friend."

"I am."

"You want both of them?"

"No, I don't want to be with Star," he says in an exasperated tone.

"You just don't me to be with her?"

"No, I just don't want you to hurt her."

"Thanks for the vote of confidence, dude."

"Well, you don't exactly have the best track record with girls," Ryker says. "And she's nice, Beckett."

"Yeah, I get it. She's nice. I'm the big bad wolf. Don't worry. It's strictly professional between us." I remember the way she breathed the word "desire" and how she puckered her lips when she thought I might kiss her, and my stomach knots.

"Good. I mean, it's what's best for the band, right?"

"Yeah, it's what's best for the band," I repeat, hoping to convince myself. After hanging up, I reach for my notebook and pen lying on the couch next to me. I scrawl the words I wrote while Star was here so I won't forget them. Then I pick up my guitar and set it in my lap. My fingers pick at the strings, and I try out the lyrics again. Closing my eyes, I picture Star's face as I sang. Her expression was a mixture of concern and curiosity. When she asked who the song was about I almost told her. There's something about her that I trust, and I know if I spend too much time with her I'll yield to her. Only, I can't afford to trust someone like that. Besides, it wouldn't be fair to her. No matter how hard I tried, in the end I know I'd hurt her. It wouldn't be intentional, but I wouldn't have a choice. There is only one path for me in this life, and it doesn't include getting close to a girl.

"Is it safe to come in?" I hear Tate's muffled voice through the door the minute I stop playing.

I set my guitar down by my feet. "Yes, come in."

The door opens and Tate pops his head in, his gaze scouring the place.

"She's gone," I reply.

"Already, huh?" Tate grins while walking inside and closing the door. "I wasn't sure what I'd walk in on."

"I told you we were just writing together. That's it."

"Yeah, but then I met her." Tate cocks an eyebrow and takes the seat next to me. His gaze lands on the sheet of paper I scrawled the lyrics on. "Is this the song you wrote together?" He snatches it up.

"Well, not really together. Star writes songs about sunny skies and happy love." I smile in spite of myself.

Tate's face grows serious. "Is this about who I think it is?"

I nod.

"Did you tell Star about her?"

"Of course not." I kick my guitar lightly with the toe of my shoe. "It's just that when Star's around I can't get Quinn off my mind. Doesn't she kind of remind you of her?"

Tate drops the sheet of paper back onto the couch and sits back. "Now that you mention it, I guess. They have the same dark hair and eyes."

"But it's more than that."

"Yeah, it's the innocence. You nailed it in the song." Tate furrows his brows. "Is that why you're not into Star? Because she reminds you of Quinn?"

"Yeah," I start to tell him he's right, and then I stop myself. I'm so not in the mood for some heart-to-heart with my older brother. "That, and she's not really my type."

"Sure she's not." Tate gives me an incredulous look.

"She's not, okay, so let's just drop it." I blow out a breath.

"Fine. I'll drop it." Tate smiles broadly. "Now, do you want to hear how that thing went tonight?"

"What thing?"

"The thing I had to go to."

I am taken aback. "You really had something to go to? I was just trying to get rid of you."

"I know." Tate's eyes darken. "That's my point. I didn't have anywhere to go, so I ended up at Mom and Dad's."

"Why did you end up there? Couldn't you find a restaurant or pub or something?"

"Call me a glutton for punishment. But actually I'm just cheap, and I knew Mom would feed me."

"You're a loser." I snort.

"Anyway, I told them about your little writing session tonight."

"You didn't."

"Oh, yes, I did." He slaps me on the thigh. "Expect a call from Mom this week. You can thank me later, little brother."

I throw a couch pillow at him.

"Is that any way to treat me after I gave you a night alone with your friend?" As he walks back toward his bedroom, my chest tightens. I picture Star's vulnerable expression; the disappointment painted on it when I told her to leave. Maybe it would have been better if Tate hadn't left us alone. Perhaps we need to have constant supervision.

11
Star

"So, how did it go?" Lola asks the minute I get back to the dorm. She's wearing sweat pants and a t-shirt, but her makeup and hair are still done up from her date with Ryker.

"Ugh." I fling myself on my bed, hoping my cheeks will cool down. They've been burning up since I left Beckett's.

"That good, huh?"

Rolling over, I press my cheek into my pillow. "Can we please not talk about it? Tell me about your date with Ryker."

"It was good." Lola bites her lip, and her face reddens.

"Where did he take you?"

"We sort of hung out here." She fidgets with the bottom of her shirt.

I giggle. "Lola, you bad girl."

"Shut up." She tries to look mad, but a smile breaks out on her face. "Like you're one to talk. You were at Beckett's apartment alone all night.

What happened?"

"We just wrote music, that's all."

"Yeah right."

I sit up, pushing the hair back from my face. "I'm being serious, Lola. Why don't you believe me?"

She shrugs. "It's just that when I told Ryker where you were, he seemed pretty sure that Beckett would try something with you."

"Why did he think that?" I'm hoping she'll say it's because Beckett has told Ryker he likes me or something.

"Because according to Ryker, Beckett tries something on every girl he gets alone with. He seems to think it's like impossible for Beckett not to."

I feel sick. "Well, then I guess I'm the one girl he can control himself around."

Lola's eyes widen. "Oh. Well, I mean, that's a good thing, right?"

I narrow my eyes at her, feeling even more stupid than before. "How is that a good thing, Lola?"

"I don't know." Lola looks so worried as she scrambles for something to say that it almost makes me feel sorry for her. "Maybe it just means that he respects you more than he does other girls."

Frustration bursts out of me like a shaken

soda. "I don't want him to respect me. I want him to want me like he does all those other girls."

Lola's mouth gapes open. "Did you seriously just say that?"

I slink back. "I'm just as surprised as you are."

Lola jumps down from her bed and walks toward me. After sitting by my legs, she rests her hand on my arm. "Who are you and what have you done with my best friend?"

I laugh and throw my head back. "I don't know what's happening to me, Lola. I've always been so practical when it comes to boys."

"Yes, I know. You went out with that dud Spencer for like three years."

"And then he cheated on me."

"Bastard," Lola mutters under her breath. "And you were always too good for him."

"I've just never felt like this around a guy before. He makes me different."

"Good different or bad different?"

"I don't know." I sigh. "But whenever he looks at me, I just want to jump into his arms and kiss him. And tonight I almost did."

"See, I knew something happened."

"But that's just it. Nothing happened. I told him I desired him, and he told me to go home."

"You what?" Lola shouts.

I run my hand over my face. "I know. I'm

such an idiot."

"Okay, okay, start from the beginning. Tell me what happened."

So I do. I spill the entire humiliating story. When I finish Lola strokes my arm, a look of pity cloaking her face. "Maybe he thought you were talking about someone else. It's not like you point blank said that you desired him."

I fix her with an incredulous stare. "C'mon, it's totally obvious what I meant. And when I first looked at him it seemed like he desired me too."

"He probably does."

"Oh, yeah, that must be why he kicked me out."

"Star, don't take this the wrong way, okay?"

I cock my head to the side, almost afraid to hear her out. "Okay," I say, drawing the word out slowly.

"I think it's probably for the best. I mean, you yourself said that Beckett makes you act differently. I know you're attracted to him, but I don't think he's the right guy for you. According to Ryker, he treats women like dirt."

"You and Ryker sure spend a lot of time talking about Beckett." I feel a little bad for how bitter I sound.

If Lola notices she ignores it. "Only because I told him where you were and he got all worried."

"About me? Why?"

"He really likes you being in the band. He doesn't want Beckett to screw it up." Lola nudges me. "Ryker says that lots of guys were asking about you after the last show. Maybe you'll start dating some hot fan."

"He really said that?" I smile. "Yeah, maybe I will." Even as I try to convince myself that's a possibility, Beckett's face emerges in my mind.

I enter the club, my heart hammering in my chest. The breeze kicks up my dress and I smooth it down. In the dim lighting I can barely make anything out.

"You're late," Beckett's annoyed voice rings out.

I squint, and see the band already on the stage for the mic check. Determined not to let my disappointment at his behavior toward me show, I cross my arms over my chest and stalk toward them. My boots stomp on the ground as I head up on the stage.

I glare at Beckett while walking toward my microphone. "Maybe if someone had picked me up I wouldn't be late."

"Fine. Ryker will pick you up for all future

gigs, okay?"

Way to dig the knife in deeper, Beckett. "Sounds great." I glance back at Ryker with a smile. "Lola says hi, by the way. She'll be here later."

"Can we get the mic check over before the show starts?" Beckett asks in a bored voice.

I turn back around. "I'm ready."

"Great," Beckett replies.

All through the mic check I study Beckett. He seems to be doing his best to avoid me the same way he did at this week's practice. I must have really freaked him out that night at his house. If only I could've kept my thoughts of desire to myself. My cheeks warm just remembering. I need to do something to make this okay again. I mean, I know that Lola's right. He's all wrong for me, but I at least want us to be friends. This whole awkward thing is too brutal. When we're finished, we all head off stage. Beckett leans against the bar in the back, taking in the room. The other guys are huddled together chatting near the stage. Mustering up all my courage, I head toward Beckett.

"Hey," I say to him, and rest my back against the bar.

He nods in response.

I consider just walking off, and leaving him to his grumpy attitude. A few people walk past us and sit down at one of the tables. I know it's nearing time for us to play. Just when I'm about to head toward the other guys, boldness takes over. "Have I done something to upset you?"

"No." Beckett slips back into the bored voice he used when we first met.

"It's just that you've been sort of weird since the night we wrote together." I hate how pathetic I sound. Trying to lighten the mood I wink. "Was I really that bad of a songwriter? Now you don't want to associate with me?"

He smiles ever so slightly. "You weren't that bad."

I nudge him with my elbow. "I promise next time I'll write all about dark clouds and sadness. No more sunny skies or flowers."

"Now you're talking." His smile is full blown now.

"Does that mean you'll give me another chance?"

He shrugs. "I guess I have to. We have a deal, remember?"

"Yes, we do." A warm feeling flutters in my stomach, and I'm happy that we're back on good terms.

Beckett's eyes rove over my body, landing on my legs. "You didn't wear the short skirt and little sandals this time."

I raise my brows. "You don't like the

dress?"

"It's not about me. It's about our male fans. I think they're gonna be disappointed that you covered your legs up with those boots."

"But you're not disappointed about it, huh?"

Beckett swallows hard. "Like I said, I'm just worried about the fans."

"Yes, your loyalty to our fans is commendable."

"Isn't it?" Beckett leans over the bar in that sexy way that looks like it belongs on a magazine cover. I glance around the room to see that it's filling up fast. Beckett grabs my elbow. "C'mon, it's almost show-time."

I nod and allow him to guide me toward the stage. Our set goes well. Only a couple of minor glitches, but considering that the audience was drinking the whole time I don't think they noticed. We end with *Can't Have,* and Beckett surprises me by heading over to my keyboard and singing into my mic with me on the last chorus. I guess he's trying to recreate the first time we sang the song together. His nearness causes my head to spin. A rush of adrenaline courses through me, and by the time we finish a lightheaded feeling has taken over.

"That was awesome!" I blurt out, feeling heat creeping into my face.

"Yeah, it was, wasn't it?"

I stand up and walk toward him. "You were amazing, Beckett."

"So were you," he says in a sincere voice that surprises me.

"Did you just say something nice about me?" I tease.

"Better not make a big deal about it or it won't happen again." He winks.

His attitude gives me a surge of courage. "I think someone's ready for their next lesson."

"Really?" He speaks in an amused tone.

I nod. "Yeah, maybe we can chat over coffee or something after we clean up tonight."

His eyes darken, and my insides wither. I can tell he's going to turn me down before he even speaks.

"Not tonight. Another time, okay?" His gaze flits over to a few over made-up girls standing near us.

"Seriously?" My stomach drops. "You're ditching me for your fan club?"

"Why? You wanna join it?" He jokes.

I don't laugh with him.

"C'mon. It was a joke."

"Whatever. I thought I saw something in you. I guess for a minute I thought you were different." I whip away from him.

"Wait." His fingers clamp over my wrist.

99

I slowly pivot on my heels, and glance over my shoulder at him.

"What do you want from me?"

"I don't want anything from you." I shake his hand off and scurry down the steps.

"Star," he calls after me, but I just keep going. Lola's right. He's not the right guy for me, and the sooner I come to grips with that, the better.

12
Beckett

I push her up against the wall, my hands skimming her waist. She reaches under my shirt and dances her fingers over my abs and chest. I kiss her harder, my tongue shooting into her mouth. A moan escapes through her lips, and it's all the invitation I need. I lower my hand, fumbling with the button on her impossibly short skirt. She thrusts her hips forward, encouraging me to continue, and her hand moves down to my zipper. Our tongues mesh together, and she pants against my mouth.

I groan with desire. "Oh, Star."

"What?" She stiffens.

Shit. Did I just say that?

"Did you call me Star?"

Yeah, I guess I did. What is her name? Candy? No, that was a different night. What the hell is this girl's name?

"Sorry, babe, what I meant was that you're my Star. My little rock star for the night." Hoping that corny line will appease her, I lean in and catch her lips in my teeth. Her button comes undone, and I rip open her skirt.

She breaks away from me. "But isn't Star the name of the girl in your band?"

Why did I have to bring home the one girl with a good memory? "It doesn't matter. You're the one I'm here with, right?"

"What's my name, Beckett?"

I groan, releasing her.

"Yeah, that's what I thought." She scrambles to put back on her skirt and close her top. "Man, my friends were right about you. I should've known better. It's just that you seemed so sweet back at the bar, I thought maybe you were different."

I run a hand over my head thinking how that's the second time tonight a girl has said that to me. Star's face fills my mind. I picture her large dark eyes framed with thick lashes, her pale face and heart shaped lips. She's the one I really wanted to bring home tonight, but I knew I couldn't do that. I'm so lost in my thoughts I don't even see what's- her- name leave. By the time I look up, my bedroom door is open. I zip back up my pants and walk out into the family room just in time to see her slip out the front door. Shaking my head, I don't even bother to go after her.

Did I seriously say Star's name while I was

making out with no-name? I've never done that before. What is wrong with me?

"Whoa, was that a friend of yours I just saw tearing down the hallway?" Tate enters the apartment, a smile on his face.

"Shut up."

He slams the door behind him. "Wanna talk about it?"

"No, I don't." I turn away from him and hurry to my bedroom. Once inside, I throw myself on my bed. I stare up at the ceiling, my hands behind my head. What is it about Star? Why do I keep thinking about her? Sure, she's different than the other girls I've been with and she does bear a striking resemblance to Quinn. But there's got to be more to it than just that. There has to be. No girl has ever messed with my mind like this before. Maybe it's because she calls me on my stuff. No one else does that. Every other girl just placates me. Or maybe it's because she's so sexy and talented. I sit up, exhaling. Man, I've got to stop thinking like that.

It was obvious tonight that if I had wanted to hook up with her she would've gladly said yes. And I was seriously tempted. But that can't happen between us for so many reasons. I have to work on my self control when it comes to her. Somehow I have to get her out of my mind. But even as I think it, I know it won't be that simple.

I successfully avoid Star at the next two weeks of rehearsals. Sure I say hi and act cordial, but I work hard not to make eye contact or encourage small talk. It mostly works because we're so busy trying to get our songs ready for the big winter festival in a couple of months. Every winter Seattle holds an all day festival for local bands to showcase their talent. All of us want to do our best. There will be lots of talent agents and producers attending, and it could be our big chance.

Besides, Ryker keeps Star occupied. They seem to have become pretty good friends. I think it's mainly because he's dating her roommate, but sometimes I feel a twinge of jealousy at the ease in which he talks with her. I wish things could be that natural between Star and me, but things are different for us. There is a chemistry with us that isn't present with her and Ryker, and I'm scared of what will happen if I allow it to spark. I know it will only result in someone getting hurt. At first I thought it was a given that it would be her, but now I'm not so sure. Either way, I don't want to find out. I've worked hard to stay away from serious relationships for a long time, and I don't plan on getting involved in one now.

I kneel down and unhook my amp after

practice. A shadow appears on the ground in front of me, and without even looking up I know it's her. I can tell by the sweet scent washing over me. It causes my pulse to race. Reluctantly I look up.

"So I was thinking that we probably need some new music to play at the festival," she says.

I stand up to face her. "Yeah, I'm working on some stuff."

"Or maybe it's time for my next lesson." Her tone is so hopeful it breaks my heart.

"Star, you don't need me to teach you how to write lyrics. I was just being a jerk before. If you want to write happy songs, that's fine with me. It's who you are. You should embrace that."

Star's face falls. "So what are you saying? That you're backing out of our deal?"

"I'm saying that we never should've made a deal in the first place. I was just playing around."

"Well, I wasn't, and I plan to hold up my end. You still haven't learned how to get close to people yet, and I plan to teach you." She lifts her chin exposing her neck, and I want to nibble on it.

All the more reason I have to put a stop to this. "I am close to people. Ryker and I have been friends forever, and my brother and I are close."

"But you're afraid to let in anyone new."

"Oh, believe me, I let plenty of new people in," I say with a light chuckle under my words so she'll catch my meaning.

105

She narrows her eyes. "I'm not talking about the girls you hook up with from your fan club. I'm talking about really letting someone in."

"Star." I step closer to her and speak softly. "I know you're just trying to help, but I don't need saving. I'm happy with how I am."

She shakes her head. "I guess I shouldn't be surprised by this. I thought you wanted to be my friend, but I should've known better. I see the way you treat the rest of the band members. I don't know why I expected it to be different with me."

"What are you talking about?"

"Oh, come on. You treat all of us like we're crap on the bottom of your shoe. Like we should all be so grateful that the amazing Beckett even graces us with his presence."

"That's not true."

"Yes, it is." She sighs. "Every once in awhile I see another side of you, and I guess I just wanted to try to draw that out. But I'm done. Don't worry. I won't hold you to your deal. We're bandmates, and that's all we'll ever be. I'm cool with that." Star whirls away from me. "Bye, Beckett. See you next week."

I watch her retreating back as she stalks out of the garage, and dread sinks into my stomach. It's weird because I miss her already. I can tell that she's serious. She's not going to try to force the deal on me, and she's not going to try to be my friend anymore. This should make me feel relieved. After all, it's what I wanted, isn't it? But I had kind of got used to her little advances and not so subtle hints. I'm not sure I'll like it when she ignores me.

"What was that about?" Ryker sneaks up on me.

"Nothing." I shake my head.

"She seemed upset."

"No, she's fine."

"Are you?" Ryker eyes me suspiciously.

I shrug. "Of course."

"Okay. If you say so."

I turn away from his intense glance, wishing he didn't know me so well. Star's wrong. Being close to people is overrated.

13
Star

When I get home from rehearsal, the dorm room is empty. I think Lola is meeting Ryker somewhere after our practice, so I know I'll be alone for awhile. Pulling my little keyboard out from under my bed, I set it on top of the covers. My emotions are so crazy right now. I know that the only thing that will soothe me is music. I kneel back down and brush my fingers over the stiff carpet until I find my folder of music. After yanking it out, I stand back up and brush off my legs. I sit on the bed and open the folder. I scan the handwritten songs, but my heart doesn't connect to anything. Beckett's right. My songs are all so happy, and right now I'm not happy.

　　　　Usually when I'm sad my first inclination is to just pretend I am happy and move on. But for some reason right now I can't do that. Beckett said that writing is therapeutic for him, and his lyrics are beautiful. Maybe I can channel some of my frustration into a haunting melody. I grab a clean sheet of paper and a pen. Then I power up my keyboard, careful to keep the volume low so I won't bother the rest of the floor. Placing my fingers on the keys, I close my eyes just like Beckett told me to. I picture his face, his body, his hands, his mouth, his tattoo, his rock hard abs. Opening my eyes, I shake my head. Okay, this is not helping.

After taking a deep breath, I close them again. This time I picture his dismissive attitude toward me; the way he acts like he's my friend one minute and my enemy the next. I allow my fingers to play around with the keys until I find the sound I like. I'm surprised that I decide on such a dark tone. Beckett has brought out a side of me I didn't even know existed. Words pop into my head, sentences strung together to relay my feelings. Reaching for the paper and pen, I scrawl the words out before I lose them. When I'm done, I drop the paper and start to play again, singing along.

The door pops open and Lola steps inside. "Hey, did you write that?"

I nod, clicking the keyboard off.

Her eyebrows lift in surprise "It's a lot different from your normal stuff."

Biting my lip, I gather the pages together and slip them into my folder. "Yeah, I was just trying out something new." I roll my neck, working out the kinks from being bent over my

109

keyboard all night.

"Beckett's influence?"

"It was definitely inspired by him," I mutter under my breath.

"Uh oh, what happened now?"

"Nothing." I wave away her words. "How was your night?"

"Good." She sits down on the edge of her bed and peels off her shoes. "Ryker said that one of his friends is interested in you."

Here we go. I know exactly where this is headed.

"Yeah, he's come to a couple of your shows, and he's been working up the nerve to ask you out. Ryker thought maybe we could double on Saturday night."

"A blind date?" I groan. "You know how much I hate those."

"I know you don't like blind dates, but I think it'll be fun." Lola has that crazy twinkle in her eyes, and I know exactly what she's doing. I've always felt like a stray cat that needs rescuing when it comes to Lola. She took me under her wing freshman year of high school, and she's made it her mission in life to protect and help me. Don't get me wrong, I think it's sweet, and she's been incredibly supportive, but sometimes I wish she'd just let me work things out on my own. I'm not that same shy girl I was when we met. I don't need her to manage my social life anymore.

"I don't know," I say.

"You haven't dated any guys since Spencer, and your fixation on Beckett isn't healthy. C'mon, I think you should go out with us."

I think back to rehearsal and how Beckett treated me, and I know she's right. Only I don't want to go on a blind date. Especially not a double date with Ryker and Lola. They are so happy together. If the guy ends up being a dud, it will be brutal.

"I'll think about it," I finally answer.

"Great." She smiles broadly.

"Don't get your hopes up," I scold her. "I didn't say yes."

"But you also didn't say no."

True.

The crisp morning air brushes over my skin. I wrap my jacket tighter around my body and walk quicker, hoping to get my circulation going. Leafy trees bend down to meet me as I take the pavement path that weaves through campus. My hair whips around my face emitting its floral scent into the air. As I turn the corner, my phone vibrates in my pocket. I pull it out and smile at the text from Lola.

Maid report: Picked your clothes off the floor.

I stop walking and shoot off a reply. **Sorry. I was running late this morning.**

You need to stop staying up all night crying over Beckett.

I was not crying.

Pouting. Same diff.

OK, Lola. C U after class. I tuck the phone back in my pocket and hurry forward. I pass a group of blond girls all giggling and chatting. Their voices are loud and I freeze when I hear a familiar name.

"So, tell me all about Beckett. Is he as good as I've heard?"

"Better," the other girl replies, and they all giggle.

My stomach churns.

"I can't believe he took you home after the show. That's like my total dream come true."

"So, don't hold out on us," another girl says. "Tell us how he was in bed."

I inhale sharply and scurry away from them, having no desire to hear the response to that question. The thought of Beckett in bed with that tall blond girl is enough to make me want to hurl. Not that I should care. He's nothing to me. Just the leader of my band, and that's all. Isn't that what I told him last night? Still, why does it bother me so much to imagine him with someone else? What is it about him? Why can't I just move on?

Walking in a speedy gait toward my class, I think over my conversation with Lola the night before. I didn't give her an answer about the double date, but now I'm thinking I should say yes. It sure beats pining after a guy I can never have. And who knows, maybe the date won't be so bad.

When Ryker introduces me to his friend Forrest, the first thought I have is that he looks nothing like Beckett. He's good looking with his blond hair, blue eyes and tanned skin, but he's more surfer boy than rocker boy. There was a time when this would've appealed to me. In fact, if I had met him a month ago I probably would've been attracted to him.

But that was before I met Beckett.

Sitting across from Forrest at the restaurant and watching him take a sip of his water, I wonder if I'll ever stop comparing every guy I meet to Beckett. It's just that I can't get the fantasy of being with him out of my mind. I've already been with guys like Forrest. Guys who wear preppy shirts, comb their hair to the side, and are devoid of tattoos or piercings. Guys who are predictable, unassuming, and never take a risk. Those guys don't get my blood boiling. They don't make me feel hot like I'm burning up with a fever, and they don't make my head swirl with dangerous possibilities. Where's the fun in that?

"I really enjoy watching you perform," Forrest says, pulling me out of my reverie.

"Oh, thanks." I smile, tearing off a chunk of sourdough bread and stuffing it into my mouth.

Lola gives me a funny look, but I just keep chewing while my thoughts keep drifting to Beckett. I try to picture him in this fancy steakhouse, and it makes me want to laugh. His jeans and tight t-shirts may not be the right attire. It makes me wonder where he'd take me on a date if we ever went out.

"When did you start playing?" Forrest asks, and again I work hard to keep focused on him.

"Oh, I've been playing since I was a kid." I take the last bite of my bread and glance out the window at the dark sky. The guy seems nice enough, but I don't feel like sharing my life story with him right now. In truth, I wish I'd never gone on this date in the first place. Going to a fancy restaurant is exactly the kind of boring thing Spencer and I did all the time. I'm in college now, I'm in a band, and I'm ready for some excitement. I think wistfully about my keyboard back home and the new song I wrote. I'd rather be playing somewhere than sitting here at a candlelit table with a white napkin draped over my lap.

"Hey, guys." I lean forward, an idea

formulating. "It's open mic night at the coffee shop. Waddya say we head there after? I have a new song I could perform."

Forrest's eyes light up, reminding me of how I feel at the prospect of hearing Beckett sing. Maybe he's looking for the same thing I am. "Sounds great," he says. "I'd love to hear it."

"Yeah, okay," Ryker agrees, grabbing Lola's hand. She just furrows her brows suspiciously at me. I squirm under the scrutiny of her gaze, wishing she couldn't read me like a book.

When the waiter brings our food, Lola leans over and whispers harshly in my ear, "What's going on with you?"

"Nothing." I shrug.

"Forrest is a nice guy. Give him a chance." She pins me with a glare.

"I'm here, aren't I?"

"Everything okay?" Ryker raises his brows while staring in our direction.

Lola smiles and straightens up. "Yeah. Just girl talk, you know?"

"Glad we weren't in on that." Ryker laughs, glancing over at Forrest.

Reaching for my fork, I look around the table. A hard knot forms in my chest when I capture a glimpse of Lola giggling at something Ryker says. Why couldn't that be Beckett and me?

Why did I have to fall for a guy who's never going to fall for me? Lifting my eyes to Forrest, I assess him. Would it really be so bad to just give him a chance? Maybe if I did it would help me get my mind off of Beckett. Noticing me staring, he flashes me a genuine smile. He's so nice it makes my heart ache. I could do a lot worse. An image of Beckett's muscular arms painted with his tattoo, his piercing eyes and crazy good voice fill my mind. *I could also do a lot better.*

14
Beckett

I barely step inside the coffee shop when I hear her voice. Instantly I recognize the clear, smooth tone, and I know it's Star. For one second I contemplate heading out, but then I catch the haunting melody, and it causes me to freeze. This is not like her usual chipper stuff. This is different, and I have to hear more. I keep walking in, allowing the door to close behind me. Careful not to let her see me, I lean against the back wall.

She's bent over the keyboard, her dark hair falling like a curtain over her face. Her slender arms move swiftly over the keys, and her lyrics wash over me.

You reeled me in like a fish on a hook

Then you threw me overboard without a single look

Now I'm sinking, I'm drowning

Alone in the water

You left me

To be pulled under

I listen with fascination. She finally did it. She reached deep down and pulled out something raw and emotional. I find myself wondering who the song is about. When she finishes, she gazes up. Her cheeks are flushed like they always are when she ends a song. Her lips are shimmery under the dim lights. As she tucks a strand of hair behind her ear, I keep myself hidden behind a cluster of people. She stands, and my eyes drop to her bare legs. Damn, she wore a skirt again. After scurrying off stage, she sits down at a table with three other people. It's then that I recognize Ryker and Lola, but I don't know who the other guy is. When I see him lean over and whisper something to Star, my insides churn. Is she on a date with that guy? Not that I care, but the guy looks like a tool. He doesn't look like someone Star would date in a million years.

Satisfied that she won't see me, I make my way to the counter and order a latte. As soon as it's ready, I feel someone nudge my shoulder. I turn around to see Star giving me a quizzical look.

"Hey, what are you doing here?" she asks.

"Same thing as you, I guess."

She looks down at my empty hands. "You didn't bring your guitar."

"Wasn't planning to play tonight. Just needed a little pick-me-up." I hold up the white paper cup. "Got a long night of writing ahead of me."

"You never cease to amaze me." She smiles.

"Why?" I ask, curious.

"It's just that I always thought rockers stayed up late drinking shots of tequila or beer or something while they wrote. Not coffee."

My chest tightens at her words. "Sorry to destroy your image of the rockstar lifestyle, but I don't drink, Star."

She nods, clearly sensing my darkening mood. "That's fine. I don't either. But I guess that's for different reasons. I'm not old enough."

The corners of my lips curl upward at her nervous ramblings. "It's fine." We move away from the counter together. "So, that song you played. Was it something new?"

Her cheeks redden. "Yeah, I wrote it the other night."

"See, I told you that you didn't need my help to become a better songwriter."

She lowers her gaze and bites her lip. "I guess not."

"It definitely wasn't like your others," I say.

"No, it wasn't." She glances up at me, and I think she might say more. But then her gaze flits over to her table and she sighs. "I better get back to my date."

"Your date, huh?" I peer over at him.

"You're seriously going out with that guy?"

"What?" Star places her hand on her hip. "He's nice. He's a friend of Ryker's."

That's when it hits me. "Ah, yes. I thought he looked familiar. He has some kind of nature name."

"Forrest."

"That's right." I fight back a chuckle. "Forrest."

Star gently smacks me in the shoulder. "Stop."

"What?"

"I can tell you're trying not to laugh at his name."

"Do you blame me?"

"Yes. Believe me, with a name like Star, I've been teased endlessly. Therefore, I never make fun of other people's names."

"Fair enough." I grin. "Well, then go back to your date with the cluster of trees and have fun."

"Nice." She rolls her eyes at me. "Good-bye Beckett."

"See ya, Star." I watch her as she makes her way back to her table. When Forrest turns to her with a grin, I have the strange urge to punch him in the face. What is it with this girl? How does she have the ability to bring out this side of me?

"So, who's the girl?" A familiar voice growls behind me.

My shoulders tighten and my insides churn. It takes all my willpower not to completely lose it. Gritting my teeth, I turn around. He looks exactly the same as the last time I saw him. His greasy hair hangs down to his ears, his dark eyes are ringed with circles, and his tall frame is lanky.

"What are you doing here, Dante? Wouldn't you be more comfortable in a bar? Or at a dealer's house?" I spit the words out.

Dante throws his arms up in mock surrender. "Just here for open mic night, man."

I glance down at his guitar with disgust. "You playing? Well, I guess I should thank you for the warning then. I'm outta here."

Dante's gaze roams over to where Star is seated. "That the new girl in your band? She looks a little familiar, like I've seen her before or something."

I know what he's saying, and it causes my blood to boil. I ball my hands into fists at my side. "You better stay the hell away from her."

Clucking his tongue, he leans toward me. "Or what, Beckett?"

I breathe in through my nose, keeping my lips together and think of Quinn. Letting him get under my skin is not a smart move. The last time I did that it ended badly for me. Without a word, I shove past him.

"You might want to stay," Dante calls from

over my shoulder. "I have a feeling things are going to get interesting."

His words shiver over my skin, and I stop in my tracks. I curse myself for showing up here tonight. It would've been better if Dante hadn't seen me with Star. I know my feelings for her are pretty complicated, and even though Dante's a complete loser he has an uncanny ability to read people. And I know he'd do just about anything to goad me. With a frustrated groan, I turn back around and try to locate a seat. As much as I don't want to watch Dante perform, I know I have to stay for Star's sake. Forrest may be her date, but when it comes to Dante I'm the only one who can protect her.

15
Star

"Oh, no," Ryker says under his breath as a tall, lanky guy walks up onto the stage.

"What?" Lola asks, her fingers lighting on his arm.

"Nothing. I'm sure everything will be fine," Ryker answers, but he's fidgeting and appears more nervous than I've ever seen him. "At least Beckett isn't here."

This causes alarm bells to ring in my head. "Beckett is here."

"What?" Ryker's eyebrows shoot up, just as the guy on stage starts playing his guitar.

"Yeah." I glance behind us and find Beckett sitting at a table near the back window. "See, he's right there."

"Oh, man." Ryker groans, running a hand over his face.

"Why? What's going on?" I ask, my throat tight. Before Ryker can answer, the guy on stage jumps to the ground in front of me with his guitar in hand. He leans toward me, singing seductively in my face. His voice is nothing compared to Beckett's, but it's not bad either. It has kind of a nice raspy quality.

"Beckett's going to lose it," Ryker says, and my body tenses at his words.

What is going on?

I scoot my chair back a little and glance over at Forrest. He's furrowing his brows, and I can tell he's as confused as I am. But this only seems to fuel this strange singer more. He bends over me still singing. It's clear that he's totally flirting with me, and I hear a few girls giggling and squealing. I know that sound. It's the same one Beckett's fan club makes when they wait for him after the shows. Clearly this guy has a fan club as well, only I can't tell why. He's not nearly as good looking as Beckett. Then again, I guess if you're into that whole grunge look he wouldn't be so bad. He reaches forward and sweeps his finger over my cheek. I suck in a startled breath.

"Dante, what the hell?" Beckett's voice crashes over me.

I freeze.

Ryker jumps up. "Beckett, man, calm down."

"Stay out of this, Ryker." Beckett shoves Dante back. "I told you to stay away from her, Dante."

"And I told you things would get interesting." Dante grins. "And now things just got interesting."

"This isn't a joke, Dante."

"You know what you're problem is, Beckett? You take everything too seriously. You need to lighten up a little."

Before I can even register what's happening, Beckett's fist slams into Dante's face. Dante flies backward, blood spurting from his nose. Ryker grunts. Lola gasps. I stand there stunned. What just happened?

"Hey, break it up!" The manager of the coffee place lumbers over. "You two need to get out of here right now!"

Beckett throws his arms up, palms exposed. "Fine with me." He stalks off, rage still evident in his face.

I glance down at Dante who is scrambling off the floor. "Man, he damaged my guitar!" He yells in a nasally tone while blood continues to leak down his face. He looks at me. "You better tell your boyfriend to watch his back."

As he stomps off, Forrest gives me a questioning glance. "Is there something going on with you and Beckett?"

"No." *At least I don't think so.*

"What the hell?" Lola runs a hand through her hair, looking confused.

I sigh, my gaze reaching for the door. "I need to go talk to Beckett."

"No, that's not a good idea." Lola rushes to my side.

"Lola's right," Ryker says. "He needs time to cool off."

I shake my head. "No, I need to talk to him now." I glance sheepishly at Forrest, quite certain he's never going out with me again. "I'm sorry."

"Star." Lola grabs my arm, but I shake it off.

"I have to do this, Lola." Without letting her protest further, I race outside. The dark night air swallows me, and I look to my right and then my left, squinting. I don't see him. He's probably long gone by now.

"Hey," a voice calls out, and I recognize it immediately. No one else in the world has that same rich, raspy tone.

I walk in the direction of the voice and see Beckett standing in the shadows. "You're still here," I say, stating the obvious.

"I just wanted to make sure Dante didn't cause any more trouble." He leans his back against the wall, and tucks his hands into the pocket of his jeans.

"What was that all about? Why were you fighting about me?" I hold my breath awaiting his answer. When he went after Dante it seemed that he was jealous and staking his claim on me. It almost scares me how much I want it to be true.

"We weren't fighting about you, Star."

"Oh." My stomach sinks. "Then what were you fighting about?"

"Dante is the lead singer of Cold Fever."

Anger courses through me. I should've known this was just some stupid band thing. "So, this is all just about a band rivalry."

"No, it's more than that." Beckett pauses, sighs. "Years ago, Dante stole away the only girl who ever meant anything to me."

I feel like I might puke. "That's why you hit him. For this other girl?"

"Yes."

"I see."

His eyes lock with mine. "No, it isn't what you're thinking."

"It's fine." I move away from him. "I need to get back inside."

"Wait." His arm juts out and his fingers circle my wrist. When I turn around, his face is serious like he's going to share something with me. But then just as quickly his features transform back into a teasing look. He offers me a lopsided smile and a wink. "Be careful. I hear the forest can be a dangerous place, especially at night."

"Real cute, Beckett." I glower at him.

"Hey, where's that pretty smile?"

I pull my arm back. "Goodnight, Beckett."

"Night, Star."

As I walk back into the coffee shop, I fight back tears. Why do I always make such a fool of myself when it comes to Beckett? When am I going to realize that he's never going to see me as anything more than another member of his band?

Lola spots me and races in my direction. "What happened? You look like you just lost your best friend."

I force a laugh and try to appear happier than I feel. "That's impossible. You're right here, silly."

Lola squeezes my arm. She knows me better than anyone. I know that she can tell I'm just putting up a good front, but she's still going to help me. "Yes, I am. And I'm never going anywhere."

"Thanks, Lola."

"Now let's get back to our dates." She guides me forward.

Ryker looks at me with concern when I sit down. "Everything okay?"

"Yeah, fine," I lie.

"Who knew there could be so much excitement in a coffee shop, huh?" Lola laughs in an attempt to lighten the mood.

"Right?" I join in. "I'm just glad I got my song in before all the chaos."

"And you were amazing." Forrest says, dropping his hand on my thigh.

I fight the urge to shake his hand off. He's a nice, good looking guy. I should want him to touch me. Only I know that I don't. The only guy I want is Beckett. But he obviously doesn't want me, so I need to move on.

"Thanks," I say. Deciding to play along, I place my hand over his.

Lola gives me an encouraging smile from across the table, and I know I've appeased everyone. We make small talk for a little while, and then I work up the courage to ask the question that has been nagging at me ever since my conversation outside with Beckett.

"Hey, Ryker, so what's the story with Dante and Beckett?"

His face pales. "Uh, they just have a lot of history, I guess."

Okay, so I'll have to try another tactic. "What about? Like did they both go after the same girl or something?"

Ryker laughs at this. "Beckett would never fight someone over a girl. In fact, in all the time we've been friends, Beckett has never been serious about any girl."

I wonder why Ryker is lying to me. Beckett said that Dante stole the only girl he ever cared about. Since Ryker and Beckett have been friends for so long, surely Ryker knows what happened. Why all the secrecy?

"Really?" I counter. "I thought Beckett had a lot of girlfriends."

"Nah, not girlfriends. He hooks up with a lot of girls. A new one every night, in fact."

This turns my stomach. "And he never gets attached to any of them?"

"No, he's not exactly picky with who he'll bring home. If the chick has two legs and is breathing, she's game."

I think about how Beckett always pushes me away. *I guess I'm the one girl he's picky about.*

16
Beckett

I can tell I've pissed Star off. She hardly even acknowledges me at practice. Not that I blame her. I'm sure she didn't appreciate me starting a fight in the middle of her date with the tree guy. It seems like maybe it's more than that though. I can't help but think that when she followed me outside at the coffee shop she was hoping I would admit to something. When she first asked if the fight was about her, I assumed it would reassure her to know that it wasn't. Only she appeared to be upset by it.

Once everyone packs up their stuff and starts heading out, I stop Star. I hate when she's mad at me, and I don't want to leave things like this.

"Hey," I approach her. "Do you mind staying for a few minutes? I liked that song you played at open mic night. I was hoping that you and I could run through it and I could get down the chords."

"Yeah, I guess." She shrugs, looking bored.

"Try to look a little less disappointed about spending time with me," I joke. "You're gonna give me a complex."

She cracks a slight smile. Then she jumps as if startled and glances down at the pocket of her jeans. "Oh, sorry. Hold on a minute." Reaching her fingers down, she yanks out her cell. After peering down at it, she presses a button and holds it to her ear. "Hey, Leo, what's up?" She turns away from me.

As I observe her talking animatedly with Leo, I wonder who he is. After a few minutes she hangs up and turns to me with an apologetic look. "Sorry about that."

"S'okay." I grin. "Leo, huh? Does this mean it's over between you and nature boy?"

She cocks her head to the side and gives me an annoyed look. "His name is Forrest, not nature boy. And Leo is my brother."

"I thought your brother was named Galileo. Isn't that what you said when we first met?"

"Well, wouldn't you go by Leo if your name was Galileo?"

"Good point."

"Anyway, I haven't talked to Leo in awhile, so that's why I answered."

"Does he live in this area?"

"No, he's still in California with my

parents."

"You left sunny California for rainy Seattle. Why?" I raise an eyebrow.

"Look at you being all inquisitive," she points out. "Maybe my lesson did do you some good."

I chuckle.

"Actually I came to Seattle because that's where Lola wanted to go to school."

"Do you do everything Lola does?"

This seems to rattle her, and she fidgets with the bottom of her sleeve. "I don't know. I guess not. We've just been inseparable since freshman year. She's the closest friend I have."

"I guess guys are different than chicks."

"What do you mean?"

"It's just that Ryker's my closest friend, but I wouldn't move somewhere just because he was going there."

"It's complicated with Lola and me, I guess." She shrugs, lowering her gaze, and I can tell she doesn't want to elaborate on this.

I clear my throat. "So, what do you say we start working on that song?"

"Sounds good." Star smiles, seemingly relieved that I didn't press her about her complicated relationship with Lola. As I pick up my guitar, Star makes her way to the keyboard. I grab a piece of paper and a pencil to jot down the chords. Star begins to play, and the musical sound fills the garage. The dark melody swims over me, and it's like I can feel Star's pain and anger that she must have felt when she wrote the song. Glancing up at her, I find myself mesmerized by the intense look on her face. I know I should be playing along with her, but I can't tear my eyes away from her. She sings through the chorus and then looks up at me with a questioning look.

"Aren't you going to play?" She asks, a teasing lilt in her voice. Her cheeks are pink, and she bites her lip in a way that drives me wild.

"I was too busy watching you." My flirty side takes over and I walk toward her, clutching the guitar to my chest. I bend over her keyboard, inhaling her fresh scent. "You're just so damn sexy when you play."

Her eyes widen, and I worry that I've gone too far. But then her lips curl into a smile and she leans toward me. "Really? I didn't know you felt that way."

"Believe me, Star. Every guy who watches you play feels that way."

Her hand reaches up tentatively and rests on my arm. The attraction is evident in her eyes, and I immediately regret my actions. It's so instinctual in me to flirt, and sometimes it's hard to keep my boundaries intact when it comes to Star. But I can't afford to start anything up with her. I push myself off of her keyboard and walk away.

Star gets up and follows me, her heels tapping. "Why do you do that, Beckett?"

I turn to face her. She looks so pure and open that I can hardly stand it.

"Is it just a game with you or something?" She throws her arms up in frustration.

"What are you talking about?"

"You do this to me all the time. You pull me in, and when you have me right where you want me, you push me away." Her lips tremble slightly, but she steadies them. "I can't take it anymore."

I shake my head, running a hand over my head. Is she saying what I think she's saying? This is becoming too real. I have to put a stop to it. "I'm sorry. I didn't mean to. It's just—" I clamp my mouth shut. I can't say what I'm thinking. That I just can't help myself when it comes to her. That I'm so damn attracted to her it kills me. That I've never had this problem with a girl before.

"It's just what, Beckett? Say it." Her words are harsher than I've heard from her before.

"I think you should go," I say softly.

"No." She crosses her arms over her chest. "Not until you say what you were about to say. I poured my heart out to you, it's the least you can do."

This stops me cold. "When did you pour

your heart out to me?"

"Oh, please. Like you didn't know that song was about you."

My heart plummets. And even though I know I shouldn't, I bridge the gap between us and thread her fingers through mine. "I didn't know it was about me, Star. I swear."

Her hands are soft to the touch, and I relish the feeling of them. Star peers up at me through her thick lashes. "You can't tell me that you don't feel something when we're together, Beckett."

"Star." I swallow hard and rest my forehead against hers.

"Why can't you just admit it?"

"Because it won't change anything," I tell her honestly, pulling back and releasing my hold on her.

"What's wrong with me?"

Her question catches me off guard. "Nothing's wrong with you."

"Then take me back to your place," she says, completely startling me.

If I thought her last statement was shocking, this one blows me out of the water. "Excuse me?" I choke.

She moves toward me in a seductive way. Something about sweet innocent Star acting seductive practically sends me over the edge, and I take a deep breath to calm my racing heart.

"Think of me as a member of your fan club."

I step backward. "I can't."

She freezes, her face falling. "Ryker says you'll hook up with any girl with two legs. I have two legs, Beckett. In fact, I've seen you ogling them at every show."

Damn, the girl has spunk. "Those girls mean nothing to me."

"And I do?"

"Yes," I breathe out. "You do."

"Then show me."

"Oh, God, Star, you don't know how badly I want to."

"Then what's stopping you?"

"It's complicated. I can't really get into it with you right now." I run a fingertip over her chin. "But trust me, it's not because I don't want to."

She swats my hand away. "That's bull, Beckett. If you wanted me you wouldn't keep turning me down." Stalking away, she scoops up her purse and sheet music and races out of the garage.

"Star!" I call after her, feeling like the biggest jerk on the planet.

She keeps running toward her car, her dark hair flying behind her like a kite.

I have no idea what just happened, but I'm pretty certain I really screwed things up big time.

17

Star

Bitter tears sting my eyes as I race back to my dorm room. I know Lola is expecting me to meet up with her and Ryker, but the only place I want to be is curled under the covers in my bed. I made such a fool of myself. What was I thinking? I've never thrown myself at a guy before. Hell, I've never even slept with a guy before. Something about Beckett brings out this other side of me. And it's not a good thing.

As I open the door to my room, shame washes over me remembering how Beckett completely turned me down. Ugh. I slam the door shut and then fling myself on my bed with my purse still strung over my shoulder. Rolling over, I groan into my pillow. The soft fabric cools my red face. I think about how I want to stay here forever. Beckett's face fills my mind, and I will the thoughts away. Man, if only there was a button in my brain where I could turn off all thoughts about him. But there isn't, and as hard as I try not to I keep reliving the night over and over in my mind.

My cell vibrates in my purse. I contemplate not picking up, but I know its Lola. She's been texting nonstop since I left rehearsal. If I don't answer soon she'll sound out a search party. Swirling my fingers inside my purse, I locate my phone and pull it out.

"Hello," I say, as I press it to my ear.

"Where are you?" Lola says. She's practically shouting over the loud noise in the background.

"In bed."

"What? I thought you were coming out with me tonight?"

"I don't want to."

"Uh-oh. Beckett strikes again, huh?" Lola sighs. "I knew this was going to happen the minute Ryker said that you stayed late with him. What happened now?"

"I don't want to talk about it."

"Come over to Ryker's apartment. He's having a party. It'll get your mind off of things," Lola offers in a chipper voice.

"No thanks. I just want to go to sleep."

"C'mon, Star. It'll be our first college party. You can't keep letting Beckett ruin all the fun for you," Lola tries to persuade me. "Remember when we first got here and we were so excited about all the fun stuff we were going to do?"

"Yeah," I reluctantly agree, prying myself from my pillow.

"Don't let him stop you from doing that."

She's right. Besides, if I sit at home moping all night then Beckett wins. Isn't that what I spent months doing after Spencer dumped me? It's time to grow up. I'm in college now. There are plenty of guys other than Beckett. "Okay. I'll be there in a few."

"Yay!" Lola squeals so loud I have to hold the phone from my ear.

When I get to Ryker's apartment and see all the people milling around, I start to have second thoughts. I don't really like parties. In fact, I only went to one in all of high school. Memories of that night burn the back of my throat, and I choke as if I've just swallowed acid. I'm about to turn around and hightail it home when Lola spots me. She waves in my direction, beer spilling out of her red plastic cup and fizzing down her arm.

"Star! You made it." She rushes toward me, a sheen of sweat on her face.

"Yeah." A guy walks past, bumping me with his shoulder. He mumbles something that sounds like an apology, but I'm not sure. I scratch the back of my neck and look around nervously. "I'm not sure this is my thing, Lola. Remember what happened last time we went to a party?"

"That was ages ago." Lola latches onto my arm, her long nails piercing my flesh. "Besides, I was there for you that night, and I will be again tonight."

I nod. If Lola's here, I'll be fine. She's always been good about looking out for me. Plus, haven't I been craving some excitement? So far college has been filled with firsts for me, and I've been traveling outside of my comfort zone a lot. "Okay. I'll stay."

Lola squeals, pulling me toward the kitchen. "Then let's get you a drink, missy."

I'm not entirely sure what Lola puts in my drink, but I know it's not beer. It has sort of a fruity taste to it. I actually like it, and I drink it thirstily. I stand next to Lola and Ryker, enjoying my drink and listening to the soft music that plays in the background. I feel a little like the third wheel, so once my drink is empty I nudge Lola. "I'm going to get a refill. You stay here. I'll be back."

"Did I hear you say you needed a refill?" A dark haired guy stands in front of me, wearing ripped jeans and a wrinkled t-shirt. I notice he has a piercing in his brow and a couple of tattoos on his arm. He's no Beckett, but at least he's not preppy like Spencer or Forrest.

Smiling, I thrust my cup into his hand. "Yes, I did."

"What would you like?"

I shrug, feeling flirty. "Surprise me."

I feel a little flutter in the pit of my stomach. *If only Beckett could see me now.*

18
Beckett

The door that leads into my parents' house springs open behind me. When I turn around I see my dad step into the garage. "Hey, son. I didn't think you were still here. Heard the band finish awhile ago."

I bend down and pack my guitar into the case. "Yeah, I'm just cleaning up."

Dad walks toward me, his shoulders slightly stooped. He's wearing jeans and a t-shirt, and his feet are bare. His hair is shorn close to his head, his face clean shaven. The tattoos on his arms are the only reminder of the man he used to be. "Tate came over the other night. Nice to have him back, huh?"

"It's fine." I shrug, standing up.

"He was saying that there are job openings at his company."

My insides churn like I was just struck with food poisoning. "You looking for a job, Dad?" I ask sarcastically.

"Nah, retirement's been good to me." He

smiles. "I was actually thinking about you."

"I'm not interested, Dad. I like what I'm doing."

Dad glances around. "Yeah, I know it's fun, but it doesn't exactly pay the bills."

I fight back the anger that wrestles to surface. "I get by."

"But if it weren't for your brother, you wouldn't be able to pay the rent."

"He tell you that?"

Dad sighs wearily. "Look, I just want what's best for you."

"This is what's best for me, Dad." I shake my head. "At least I'm still following my dream. I'm not abandoning it the way you did."

"You know why I had to, son."

"Yeah, I do, and that's why I work so hard to make sure no one gets in my way."

Dad frowns. "I don't regret my choices, son."

"I know, but I'm not like you, Dad." I pick up my guitar case. "I gotta take off."

"Why don't you come have dinner this Saturday night? Tate's coming over."

"I'm playing this Saturday night." I glance up at him. "Why don't you guys come see us?"

"Um..." Dad scratches the back of his neck, and I know exactly what's coming. "Maybe another weekend."

"Sure." I shrug like I don't care, and then turn away. "See ya later, Dad."

"Bye, son."

As I head to my car, the crisp night air circles me. I throw my guitar in the backseat and slide into the driver's side. As I pull away from the curb, loud music spills from the speakers, dulling my senses. Dad's words play in my mind, reminding me of why it's so important to keep Star at a distance. I've never worried about a girl getting under my skin before, but there's just something about Star. I know that if I let her in I won't want to let her go. She's the type of girl that a guy would give everything up for. Only I can't afford to give anything up. I have to keep focused if I want to make it.

I turn my car away from my apartment and toward Ryker's. The last thing I want to do is talk to Tate right now. Besides, I need to talk to Ryker about kicking Star out of the band. I'm sure he'll understand if I tell him how I feel. He's already made it clear that he doesn't want me messing with her. I park along the street in front of Ryker's place. A few people stand outside smoking. I pass them by, batting away the plumes that fill the air. The smell turns my stomach. It reminds me of the way my dad used to smell when I was a kid. I hated the way the scent lingered on his fingers, his skin, his hair.

Taking the corner, I walk up the cement path shadowed with trees. When I reach the stairs I spot a couple sitting on the steps, red solo cups in hand. My chest tightens. I sidestep past them and climb the stairs. The minute I reach his door I know that he's got a party going on inside. Loud laughter and chatter spill from under the door. I reach out and jiggle the knob. Sure enough, it's unlocked. I push it open, and my suspicions are confirmed. People are jam packed in Ryker's small apartment that he shares with Pierce. A couple makes out on the couch, and there are a few guys chugging beer in the kitchen. I finally catch sight of Ryker across the room chatting with Lola, and I start to stalk toward him. But then I catch a whiff of honeysuckle scent, and I pause. Glancing down at the couch, my heart sinks. I didn't recognize her at first because I wasn't expecting her. Star is the girl making out with some strange guy on the couch. His hands tangle in her hair, and when they separate she giggles in a way that indicates she's had a few too many. When I see her heavy lidded eyes I have the strange urge to punch the guy in the face. Can't he see that she's drunk? What kind of guy takes advantage of a girl in this condition? I force down the memories of all the times I've done it.

"Star," I say.

Her head whips in my direction. Lipgloss is

smeared up her face, her hair mussed. Anger swirls inside of me. She looks so hot, and I'm angry that I wasn't the one who made her look like that. Her mouth widens in surprise. Then she lets out another giggle and sways slightly to the side. The guy she's practically lying on top of reaches out to steady her, but I swat his hand away and latch on to her arm.

"C'mon, Star," I say gruffly, yanking her up.

She fights me off. "Let go of me. I'm having fun with…" her voice trails off and she furrows her brows.

"You don't even know his name, do you?" I ask as if I'm annoyed, but the truth is that it's all a little amusing.

"Yes, I do." She scrunches up her forehead in concentration. "Joseph."

"Jonah, but close enough." The guy sits up, smiling at Star.

"This isn't like you," I say, hoping to appeal to her sensible side.

She shoves away from me and her body wavers.

"Whoa, there," I say putting out my arms.

After regaining her balance, she tries to move away from me. "You hardly even know me."

"I know enough."

"So, is this guy your boyfriend or something?" Jonah squirms on the couch, looking uncomfortable.

Star glares at me. "No, he doesn't want anything to do with me."

"That's not true."

She opens her mouth like she's going to say something, but then a funny look passes over her face. She leans her head forward, and then I know exactly what's happening.

"Star? Are you okay?" I ask.

"Bathroom," she sputters.

I nod, understanding. Clutching her hand, I guide her toward Ryker's small bathroom located directly off the family room. The minute we get inside she falls to her knees and retches into the toilet. I reach out and sweep the hair from her face, holding it tightly in my hand as she throws up again. She wipes her mouth with the back of her hand and glances over her shoulder at me. She looks embarrassed.

"Sorry," she mumbles.

"You don't drink often, do you?"

"Never."

"It's okay. We've all been there." I rub her back.

"Thanks." Star scrambles to stand up.

"Here, I'll help you." I wrap my arm around her waist and hoist her up. "Clean up and then I'll take you home."

"Why are you doing this?" She asks.

I shrug. "It's what friends do."

"We're friends?"

"Of course." I walk out of the bathroom, closing the door softly behind me. Ryker spots me, and his face pales. I stalk toward him, anger seeping through my veins. "I can't believe you, man."

"It's just a little party. It's not a big deal." Ryker says.

"It is a big deal. Did you see how drunk Star is? She's in the bathroom cleaning up puke as we speak."

"So she had a little too much to drink. It's not the end of the world."

I stick my face in his. "This is exactly what I didn't want to happen. I have rules for a reason."

"Maybe I'm tired of living by your rules, Beckett. Sure I'm in your band, but that doesn't mean you get to run my life."

His words startle me. I step back from the force of them. "We've been friends a long time, man. I thought you understood. Maybe I was wrong."

"Look, Beckett." His tone is softer now. "Let's talk about this later, okay?"

"Oh, we'll talk about it later, because whether you like it or not I have rules for the members of my band, and there are consequences when those rules are broken."

"Rules?" Star's voice sounds behind me. "What rules?"

"I'll explain later," I say to her.

"Rules, shmules," she rolls the words around in her mouth and then laughs like it's the most amusing thing ever.

Man, she's worse off than I thought.

"I need to get you home, Star."

"You're not taking her anywhere," a female says.

I turn around to see Star's best friend standing next to Ryker. Since I'd been so focused on my anger and Ryker, I hadn't noticed her before. "She needs to go home, and no one here is in any condition to take her."

"I'll be fine, Lola," Star says, slurring her words.

"I trust you'll be a perfect gentleman?" Lola raises her brows at me.

"Hey, I'm not the one who brought her to some party and let her get hammered and hook up with a stranger," I point out.

Lola narrows her eyes and crosses her arms, scaring me. When a chick looks like that it can't be good. "And I'm not the person who upset her so badly tonight that all she wanted to do was get hammered and hook up with a stranger."

I know I upset Star tonight, but I didn't realize just how badly. "Okay, you got me," I say. "So, let me make it up to her."

"Just be careful," she speaks through gritted teeth.

I nod to Lola and Ryker. Then I grab Star's hand and lead her out of the apartment. She stumbles at my side, so I grip her hand tighter and try not to think about how much I like the feeling of her hand in mine. We weave through couples until we reach the front door. A cold breeze smacks me in the face when we step outside. Star leans into me, so I snake my arm around her waist to steady her. I hold her to me as we make our way down the stairs. Her hair brushes against my shoulder, and my heart rate speeds up. I am enjoying this a little too much.

"You doing okay?" I ask once we reach the bottom of the staircase.

She nods and flashes me a lazy smile. Her eyes are mere slits on her face, and her grin is devilish. I clear my throat and force my gaze away.

"My car's this way." I yank her in the direction of it and move swiftly. The faster I get her home, the better. Didn't I come here to talk to Ryker about kicking her out of the band? How did it end with Star in my arms? Nothing about the way I act around this girl makes any sense to me.

After opening the passenger side door, I help Star sit down and then race to my side. I slide in and start the engine. After pulling away from the curb, I glance over at Star and notice that she changed out of her jeans and t-shirt that she had on earlier. Now she wears a little skirt and long sleeved shirt. I swear the chick is trying to kill me with those legs.

"See something you like?" Star's voice startles me, and my face goes hot. On the one hand I'm embarrassed that she caught me staring at her legs, on the other hand I'm completely turned on by her brazen statement.

Afraid of what I might say, I just press my lips together and stare back out the front window. I keep my gaze trained on the ground in front of me, my arms gripping the steering wheel with a death grip. I need to get her home. If she keeps flirting like this I fear I won't be able to control myself. What possessed me to offer her a ride home?

A vision of Quinn fills my mind, and then I know exactly why I have to do this; why I have to do everything in my power to keep Star safe. If what Lola said is true, then it's my fault Star was at the party in the first place. That makes me just as bad as Dante. Just the thought of that guy puts a sour taste in my mouth. The last guy I ever want to be compared to is Dante, so I know I have to make this right.

The car ride is silent. In fact, after a few minutes I assume Star has passed out. But when I glance back at her she is just staring at the window with a glazed expression. It's clear that she's still pretty out of it. When we pull into the college campus, my stomach twists into knots. I know I can't just leave her in the parking lot. That wouldn't be safe. So, I'll have to walk her to her dorm room. Although, the truth is that won't be safe either.

"Thanks for the ride," Star says, slurring her words. She fumbles with the door handle for a few seconds before successfully opening the door.

"I'll walk you up." I follow her.

"So, was this your big plan? You wanted to get me drunk and have your way with me?" She circles her arms around my neck and bats her eyelashes.

Damn, this is not going to be easy for me. I swallow hard, prying her arms off of my neck. "No, believe me. This was not my plan." I turn from her and keep walking forward.

"Then why did you show up at the party?" She walks faster until we are side by side again.

"I didn't know there was a party. I just wanted to talk to Ryker."

"Oh. So you didn't go there for me?" I hear the disappointment in her voice and my stomach drops. If only she didn't wear her heart on her sleeve.

"No, but I'm sure glad I showed up when I did."

"Why?" Suddenly her tone switches from disappointment to anger. "You ruined my night. I was having a good time with Joseph."

"Jonah," I correct her, a smile playing on my lips. She sure is cute when she's mad like this. "And he was an idiot."

"He was not." She turns a corner, and I follow her. "He was cute and nice, and he wanted me." She stops in front of a dorm room that I'm assuming is hers.

"Star," I say softly. "He was drunk and he was taking advantage of you."

"Are you saying that a guy could only want me if he's drunk?" She shakes her head. "Wow, you really are a piece of work, you know that?" With trembling fingers, she digs inside her purse trying to locate her keys.

"Calm down. That's not what I said."

She yanks her keys out, but they slip from her fingers and crash to the ground.

"Here." I lean down to grab them. "Let me help you." After unlocking the door, I push it open. "Are you going to be okay tonight?" I ask before she steps inside.

Star searches my face for a minute. "Why

are you being so nice to me all of the sudden?"

"I didn't realize I was such a jerk the rest of the time?" I joke.

"You know what I mean."

"I told you it's because we're friends."

"Friends, huh?" She inches closer to me and I smell the alcohol on her breath. It reminds me of why I have to keep my distance. "Is that all we are?"

"Star," I start to speak, but then she loses her balance and topples into me. I catch her in my arms.

Giggling, she peers up at me. "Sorry."

"I'll help you inside." I guide her into her dorm room. Once inside, I take in the two beds pushed against opposite walls. It's obvious which side belongs to Star and which one belongs to Lola. Star's is clearly the messier one with the posters of bands tacked to the wall and the bed that's unmade. I may not know Star and Lola that well, but I know that Star is totally scatterbrained and unorganized, and from my few encounters with Lola I can tell that chick is completely anal about everything. I feel for Ryker, I really do. High maintenance is not my thing.

Star is still struggling with her balance, so I deposit her on her bed. Before I can pull away, she grips the collar of my shirt and pulls me down toward her. My pulse quickens as I catch a whiff of her intoxicating scent.

"How did you know which bed was mine?" she asks.

"Lucky guess." I smile, trying not to think about how close her lips are to mine.

"Why don't you stay?"

I shake my head. "I can't."

"Seriously, what is your problem?" She releases my collar and blows out a frustrated breath.

"I'm sorry, but I'm not going to take advantage of you right now."

"So, are you saying that you've never been with a drunk girl before?"

"Of course I have, but you're different."

She seems shocked at my words. "How?"

I kick myself for saying that, and my first inclination is to derail the conversation and hit the road. Then I look into her glazed eyes and throw caution to the wind. Hell, she won't remember this conversation tomorrow anyway. "I don't know. There's just something about you. Something special. You make me feel things that no other girl has before and it scares me."

Her eyes widen. "Why does it scare you?"

I sit next to her on the bed and take her hand in mine. "All I've ever wanted is to be a famous musician like my dad was. I can't let anything get in the way of that. I don't want to have to give up my dream, ever."

"Who says you'll have to give it up?"

"Do you want to know why my dad left his band?"

Star nods.

"Because my mom got pregnant with Tate. Dad's band was just about ready to leave to go on a huge tour when she found out. My dad had a choice to make, and he chose to stay with my mom. They got married, had a family, and he never looked back."

Star grimaces. "So you're worried that I'll get knocked up and force you to give up on music? That's ridiculous, Beckett."

"No, that's not it." I drop her hand, wishing I could articulate my feelings when I speak as well as I do in my songs. "I've never understood how my dad could choose a woman over his lifelong dream. But then I met you, and I could tell that you were the kind of girl a guy would give everything up for."

"I would never ask you to do that though."

I want to believe her. I want to just throw caution to the wind, sweep her up in my arms and see where this takes us. Only I know that we can't predict the future. If I go forward with this, there may come a point where I'll have to choose. That's a chance I can't take.

"It's just not that simple. I'm sorry."

"Was it that simple with the other girl you told me about? The one Dante stole from you?"

Horror fills me, and I wish I'd never mentioned that. "That's a completely different situation."

"How so?"

"I can't talk about it." Unnerved, I stand up. I'm not ready to talk about Quinn with her. "I really should go."

Star presses her lips together and turns away from me.

"Get some rest," I say, as I walk out the door. While I walk down the hallway, I feel a sense of dread. Why did I share so much with her? What was I thinking? I really hope that she doesn't remember all of this in the morning. If she does, I'm afraid I just made a horrible mistake.

19
Star

Light pierces my eyes, and my head pounds. I attempt to sit up, but I head hurts too bad. Groaning, I press my face into the pillow savoring the cool feel of it on my cheek. My stomach rolls, and my mouth fills with moisture. I swallow hard, hoping I won't throw up. That's the last time I drink too much.

"Morning, Sunshine," Lola trills.

Keeping my face in my pillow, I bat away her words with my arm. "Go away."

"I brought you something."

I feel the bed slope from Lola's weight as she sits next to my legs.

"Is it a gun? Are you going to put me out of my misery?" I tease without lifting my head.

"No, it's not a gun." Lola laughs. "But it will make you feel better."

Skeptical, I lift my head and peek out of one eye. In her hand she holds a cup with fizzy clear liquid. "What is it?"

"Alka Seltzer. It'll settle your stomach."

I pry myself off the pillow and sit up. "Why'd you let me drink so much last night?"

Lola shoves the cup into my hand. It's cold against my warm, sweaty palm. "I'm sorry. I was hanging out with Ryker. I didn't realize how much you'd had."

"That's okay. It's not your job to babysit me." I take a sip, and carbonation fizzes up my nose.

"No, apparently that job has now been handed over to Beckett," Lola says bitterly.

At the sound of Beckett's name, a flood of memories assault me and I feel even sicker than I did before.

"What happened when he brought you back here?"

I drink the last of the medicine, hand it back to Lola and then drop my head back down. "I don't wanna talk about it."

Lola's face reddens in anger. "He better not have tried anything on you."

"Don't worry. He was a perfect gentleman," I respond sourly.

"Well, good." Lola stands up.

"How is it good, Lola? The guy shows up at the party and pulls me off of Joseph, who I was having a great time with, by the way. Then he forces me to go home, but it's not because he wants to be with me or anything. It's because we're friends." I use air quotes around the word friends.

Lola scrunches her forehead together in deep thought. "I think his name is Jonah."

"Whatever."

Lola giggles. "You're mad that Beckett took you away from a guy whose name you don't even know? Wow, this is certainly a new Star."

"I'm just so tired of Beckett's mixed signals, that's all."

"Hey, I get it. I've been telling you to stay away from him for weeks."

"Only that's impossible, Lola."

"Clearly. Especially since the guy has it bad for you."

"What?"

"Oh, please. It's totally obvious. Even Ryker sees it." Lola drops the glass on my dresser and then heads back to my bed. After sitting down, she turns to me. "But Beckett has a lot of baggage, Star."

"Yeah, I can see that." I raise my brows. "Did Ryker tell you what it is?"

She shakes her head. "No, I get the feeling that it's pretty private."

"I wish I knew what it was."

"I just want you to be careful, okay?"

"Of course." I nod. "Safety is my middle

name."

Lola gives me a funny look, her gaze taking in my chaotic side of the room. "Well, it certainly isn't cleanliness, we know that."

"Shut up." I slide under my covers, pulling them up over my head.

All week I mull over my conversation with Beckett. I know I should be happy that he admitted he has feelings for me, but the truth is that it's just made everything worse. Knowing he likes me but can't act on it is torturous. That's why on Thursday night I just can't bring myself to go to rehearsal. I don't think I can handle being that near to him, knowing how he feels. It was difficult enough being around him before I knew. So I text Ryker to tell him I'm sick, and then hide out in my dorm room.

Lola is at a study session, so I know I won't have to explain myself to her right now. I don't want to leave the dorm to get food, so I raid my stash of candy. After stuffing my face with a snickers bar and way too many gummy bears, I change into my favorite pair of yoga pants, sit on my bed and play around on my keyboard a little. But I can't find any inspiration. My mind just keeps returning to the words that Beckett spoke to me the other night.

It's weird how secretive he is about the girl Dante stole from him. I feel like she's the reason he can't open up to anyone else. If only I could get him to open up about her. However, I know that's a losing battle. It's obvious that he's never going to talk about her with me. And even though Ryker and Beckett's relationship is complicated, it's clear that Ryker is loyal to Beckett. I know he won't tell me anything. And it's not like I can ask Beckett's brother about it. So, that means I may never know the whole story. Frustration burns through me. If only there were some way I could convince Beckett that I'm different from the other girl and that our situation is different from his parents. It just seems like a tragedy to me to not give our relationship a chance.

I'm not ready to entirely give up on him. I ponder how weird it is that I care more about getting together with Beckett than I did about Spencer breaking it off with me. I've never felt like this about anyone before, and that's why I can't just let it go.

A thought strikes me like the lighting of a match. *Dante.* He's the only other person who knows the story, and I bet he'd be delighted to share it with me. I jump out of bed and scoop my jeans off the floor. After changing into them, I slip on a pair of shoes, run a brush through my tangled hair and then head out.

The minute I get outside I have a nagging thought that this is a terrible mistake. If Beckett ever finds out I went in search of Dante he'll kill me. Even so, I can't make myself turn back around. This is something I have to do. I have to know what happened to Beckett to make him not trust anyone; to make him pull away from everyone who cares about him.

I have no idea where Dante hangs out, but I do know that the one time I saw him was at the coffee shop, so I head there first. If he's not there, maybe someone can direct me to him. The scent of coffee and pastries waft under my nose when I enter, and my stomach growls. I guess candy wasn't a good enough dinner for me.

After scouring the shop and realizing that Dante isn't here, I decide to order a sandwich. After ordering, I lean over the counter toward the barista. He was the same guy working the last time I played. "Hey, remember the other night when those two guys got in a fight?"

"Dante and Beckett? How could I forget?" He asks with a slight chuckle. "Those two are always getting into it."

I bite my lip as the nagging feeling returns. I know I should just forget this whole thing, but I've come too far now. "Yeah, that's right. Any idea where Dante might be tonight?"

"I'm not his personal secretary." The guy

jokes.

I laugh lightly, fighting back my irritation. "Right? Yeah, I get that. I just wondered if you knew where Dante normally hung out."

"Why are you looking for Dante?" The voice behind me causes me to practically jump out of my skin.

Dread descends into my gut as I slowly pivot on my heels. "Beckett? How come you aren't at rehearsal?"

His face is hard, his lips a thin line. "Not everyone was there, so we ended early."

"Oh. I was just picking up dinner."

"You don't look sick." Beckett speaks methodically, tapping his finger on his chin.

I feel sick now.

"Do you want to explain to me why you missed rehearsal and now you're here looking for Dante?" he asks.

Nervously I move away from the line. My sandwich is put up on the pick-up counter, so I snatch it up. "Um…" I can't come up with anything.

"Look, I have rules for the members of my band. No drinking and no drugs. The other guys all know that. I never bothered to tell you because you didn't strike me as the partying type."

My body goes numb. "I'm sorry about the other night. That was a one-time thing, I promise."

"Then why are you looking for Dante? Do you use drugs?"

"No." I shake my head vehemently. "Why? Is Dante a drug dealer?"

"You tell me. You're the one looking for him."

"Not for drugs." I run a hand through my hair, wishing I had listened to that nagging voice in my head.

Beckett raises an eyebrow. "Then why?"

"I just wanted to talk to him, that's all."

"About what?"

I take a deep breath. At this point truth is my best option. "I wanted to find out what happened between the two of you, okay?"

Beckett moves closer to me, and lowers his voice. "If you want to know something, you need to come to me."

Annoyed, I throw up my arms. "I have, but you refuse to tell me anything."

"That's because it's none of your business," he growls.

My heart stops, and all the fight withers inside of me. I drop my gaze. "You're right. I'm sorry." Without looking him in the eye, I clutch my sandwich in my hand and turn away. I think I've squeezed the bread so hard it's probably inedible at this point. As I make my way to the door, Beckett stops me.

166

"Star," he calls out.

My spirits lift, and I whirl around.

"I've talked to other guys about last weekend, but I trust that you won't let that happen again."

"Don't worry. I'll abide by your rules from now on." I start to walk away, but then stop. I won't let him get the last word in this time. "Beckett?"

"Yeah?"

"I trust that you'll stop butting into my life as well. I don't need you show up every time I'm with another guy and try to rescue me, okay?"

"Fair enough." His tone and expression give away nothing.

With a subtle nod, I scurry off so he won't see how much this conversation is tearing me up inside.

20
Beckett

I feel bad about how harsh I was with Star at the coffee shop, but she shouldn't have gone behind my back to look for Dante. I mean, what gives her the right to do that? Obviously if I didn't want to tell her about Quinn, then there was a reason. Besides, didn't I warn her about Dante? My blood boils thinking of what she might have found out. Who knows what he would have said about Quinn. That guy is a total loser. He's manipulative and vindictive. Star has no idea what kind of guy he is.

For the two weeks following the awkward encounter, Star ignores me. Not that it matters. The entire band is giving me the cold shoulder. I'm guessing they're upset at how hard I came down on them about the party at Ryker's. Maybe I did go a little overboard, but they all know my rules. And they all know why I have them. It's a matter of trust and respect, really.

Now Star is gone. She and Lola went home

for Thanksgiving week. I'm hoping that when she returns she'll have a better attitude and we can get back on track. The December festival is only weeks away, and we need to be on our game. This festival means a lot to me and the last thing I need is for it to be ruined because of all this drama. In fact, this is exactly what I was worried about when Ryker first mentioned bringing a girl into our band. If only I hadn't given in. If only the girl hadn't been Star.

I pick up my guitar and rest it in my lap. Leaning my back against the couch cushions, I prop my bare feet up on the coffee table. I strum the guitar and wait for inspiration to hit me. My goal is to write at least one more song for the festival, and I need to get going on it.

"Hey." Tate enters the room wearing ripped jeans and a wrinkled t-shirt. He sits down on the recliner, takes in my appearance and turns his nose up in disgust. "Dude, put on some clothes."

I glance down at my body. "It's not like I'm naked."

"You're only wearing boxers, man." Tate averts his gaze.

"Jealous because I look so much better than you do in your boxers?" I joke.

"You wish," he banters back. "So, are you coming to Mom and Dad's with me today?"

I groan. "I don't think so."

"Seriously? It's Thanksgiving."

"So?"

"So, you can't stay home and mope around all day."

"I'm not moping around." I rest my guitar on the ground, propping it against the side of the couch.

"Dude, close your legs!" Tate covers his eyes with his hand.

"Jealous again, huh?" Chuckling, I adjust myself.

"Just cover it up." Tate splays his fingers and peeks out of one eye. Then he sighs and drops his hand. "You've been moping around ever since you and Star had that fight."

"I have not."

Shaking his head, Tate says, "I don't know why you can't just admit that you like her."

"I did that, and look where it got me."

"Yeah, you told her you liked her but that you couldn't be with her because of all your excessive baggage, but then you didn't tell her what it was."

"I told her some of it."

"But not all."

"That doesn't give her the right to go behind my back to figure it out."

"Yeah, I don't know why she just didn't ask you, since you were such an open guy," Tate says sarcastically.

"It's personal, and it's none of her business." I bristle.

Tate leans over, resting his elbows on his knees. "Beckett, I'm only saying this because I'm your brother and I care about you, so don't take it the wrong way, okay?"

Nervous, I shift uncomfortably on the couch. Rarely does my brother speak to me like this. I spread out my arms, urging him on. "Continue."

"You need to get over yourself and grow up."

"You're one to talk," I mutter under my breath.

"Look, I know I've made a lot of mistakes, but I've learned from them. I only want the same for you." Tate pauses. "You walk around with this major chip on your shoulder and you shut everyone out. It's time to let someone in."

I have an eerie sense of déjà vu. "You sound like Star."

"Smart girl." Tate grins. "I know you're scared, Beckett. She's the first girl that's gotten under your skin like this, and you're afraid to let your walls down. But trust me, it'll be worth it if you do."

"I can't."

"Why not?"

"You know why, Tate." I reach for my guitar again. "Besides, I need to focus on my music. You of all people know what happens when you let something get in the way of your dream."

"That was totally different, and you know it."

"Was it? You, Dad, even Quinn all learned the hard way. I'm not planning to do that." Settling the guitar in my lap, I begin to play, signaling the end of the conversation.

Tate gets up and walks toward me. "Okay, I'll leave you alone about Star on one condition."

I stop playing and look up at him. "What?"

"Come with me to Thanksgiving dinner."

"You can't be serious."

"Mom and Dad really want to see you."

"Sure they do," I say disbelieving.

"Beckett, you need to stop being so hard on them."

"Why?" I ask through gritted teeth. "They don't support me at all."

"But its Thanksgiving, and they want to see you. C'mon. Do it for me at least. I don't want to go there and hear them bitch about you not showing up the whole time."

I laugh bitterly. "Fine, but only because you give me a place to live, and I sort of need to stay on your good side."

"Hey, I'll take it." Tate shrugs. "Now go get dressed. We leave in fifteen."

"What's wrong with what I've got on?" I smirk. "My female fans would pay money to see me in this."

Tate shakes his head in disgust. "Just get dressed."

"If you insist." I stand up, laughing. As I head into my room, I wiggle my butt at Tate. "C'mon, you have to admit, it is nice, huh?"

Tate puts his head in his hands and groans, but not before I see a small smile pass over his lips. After entering my room, I change into a pair of jeans and a white wife-beater tank. When I go back in the family room, Tate gives me a funny look.

"That's what you're wearing?"

"Would you rather me change back into my boxers?"

"Okay, let's go."

I wish I had a camera ready to capture the surprised look on Mom's face when she opens the door to find me standing on the porch.

"Beckett, you came?"

"Yeah, he made me." I point to Tate, who gives me a warning look.

Mom presses her lips together. "Whatever

the reason, I'm glad you're here." She envelops me in a hug, her familiar floral scent washing over me. I feel nostalgic for a minute, memories of mom embracing me when I was little boy filling my mind. But when she pulls back, I catch her eyes skimming over my attire in a disapproving way. I'm reminded that I'm not a little boy anymore, and my mom and I are no longer close. While Mom greets Tate, I step inside the cozy house I grew up in. I remember when I was a kid Dad would show me pictures of the lavish hotels he stayed in when he was in the band. Afterward, I felt so disappointed looking around our small twelve hundred square foot house, realizing everything my dad had given up. My dad had a life everyone dreams of, and he gave it all up to live in a small house and raise a family. Who does that?

"Beckett?" Dad steps into the family room, his eyebrows raised in surprise. "Glad you could make it, son."

I nod, grateful when Tate and Mom join us.

"Can I get you boys something to drink?"

"Vodka on the rocks," I say just to stir things up.

Mom frowns. "Since when did you start drinking?"

"I am twenty-one, Mom. That means it's leg-al." Noticing how tense her shoulders have become, I feel a little guilty for taking the joke this far. So I shrug. "I don't really drink, Mom. I was just teasing. I'll have a soda."

Dad exhales. I don't dare look at Tate. It's not like I have to see him to know he doesn't approve of my joke, especially since he's the main reason we don't drink in this house. The tension is so thick you can cut it with a knife. For the next hour or so, Dad, Tate and I make small talk in the family room while Mom finishes dinner. My stomach growls at the scent of turkey and spices. Finally Mom announces that dinner is ready, so we all file into the small dining room.

Dad whistles after taking in the spread. He places a hand on Mom's arm. "This looks delicious, honey."

"Thanks." She leans over and kisses him softly on the cheek.

Ignoring them, I pull out a chair and sit down. Tate takes the chair next to mine and Mom and Dad sit across from us. Silence descends on the table as food is passed and everyone dishes up. The food is delicious, and I eat greedily without saying a word. It is the first home cooked meal I've had in forever. Mostly I eat take out or grilled cheese sandwiches. I make a mean grilled cheese, which is good thing since it's pretty much the only thing I cook. Glancing up at Mom and Dad, I see them giggling together and touching affectionately. They've always been like this. It used to embarrass me when I had friends over.

Dad's words from the other evening play in my mind. He said that he never regretted his choice, and the truth is that he has always seemed happy with his life. Even though I've never understood it, he does seem to be. My thoughts flit to Star, and I wonder how her Thanksgiving is going. Picturing her sweet face and rocking body, I contemplate sending her a text, or giving her a call. As much as I hate to admit it, I have missed her over the last couple of weeks. And maybe allowing Star in won't ruin everything. Dad seems happy. Then again, maybe he would've been happier had he stayed in the band. We'll never know. And I'm not Dad. I want different things out of life. Forcing myself to abandon thoughts of Star, I take another bite of food.

21
Star

"You're enjoying school so far?" Mom asks as she passes the mashed potatoes to me.

I nod, unable to speak past the mouthful of turkey.

"Have you made any new friends?"

Beckett's face flashes in my mind and my face warms. "A couple." I still haven't told my parents about the band, and I don't plan to.

"Why is your face all red?" Leo teases me. He sits to the right of me, and nudges me in the side with his elbow.

"It's not." I scoop potatoes onto my plate.

"I think someone has a boyfriend," he says in a sing-song voice, reminding me of when we were little kids. Even though Leo's practically a grown up now, sometimes he can be so immature.

"No, I don't." I shove the bowl of potatoes into Leo's hands a little too forcefully, hoping he'll take the hint.

"That's good, because you should be

focusing your energy on school," Dad interjects, and I'm not at all surprised by his words. Dad would keep me locked in my room for eternity if he could. He never wants me to date at all.

I eat in silence for a few minutes, my mind whirring with images of Beckett. When I came here for the week, I assumed it would be the perfect opportunity to get my mind off of him. Only something about this place makes me think of him more. I feel so suffocated in my hometown. When I'm in Seattle with Beckett and the band I feel a freedom I've never experienced. Before coming here I confided in Lola that I was thinking of dropping out of the band. It's just so awkward between Beckett and I that I figured it was for the best. But the more I ponder that, I know I can't do it. I love being in the band. It's the most fun I've ever had. I can't let go of it. Not now.

"What kinds of things do you and Lola do for fun?" Mom takes a sip of her red wine.

My stomach twists. I decide to start small with my parents – baby steps. "We go to this coffee shop near campus a lot. They have open mic nights and sometimes I perform there."

"That's nice," Mom says in her placating voice while setting her glass down. "As long as your music doesn't take you from your studies I'm okay with you dabbling in it a bit."

Nodding, I pick my fork back up. I feel a

little guilty for not telling them about the band, but after her last statement I realize that I can't. My parents would totally freak out if they knew. When I lean down to take another bite, my cell vibrates in my pocket. For a brief moment, I imagine that it's Beckett. Then I glance down and see that it's Lola. Of course Beckett wouldn't text me. What was I thinking?

How is it going?

Brutal, I respond.

Did u tell them about the band?

No. Did u tell ur parents about Ryker?

What do u think?

I almost laugh out loud. Lola's parents are really rich and have high hopes of their daughter snagging a doctor or lawyer. They would not be excited that she's dating a guy who is majoring in communications because he has no idea what he wants to be other than a musician.

"What are you doing?" Leo leans over my shoulder.

"Nothing," I mumble, covering my phone with my hand and shoving it back into my pocket.

By the time dinner is over, I'm so stuffed I feel like I'll have to be rolled out of the dining room. My mind travels back to thoughts of Beckett and I wonder where is today. Did he go to his parents' house or did he and Tate stay home? It's funny because even though we practice in his parents' garage, I've never seen them. Sometimes I can hear them inside the house, or see their cars in the driveway, but they never come out and say hi. Clearly their relationship with Beckett is complicated. Then again, it seems that everything with Beckett is complicated.

I'm so glad when Thanksgiving week is over and Lola and I are back in Seattle. As we unpack our suitcases in our dorm room, Lola goes on and on about how overwhelming her parents are and how awful her older sister is. Not that she needs to tell me any of this. I've spent enough time with her family to know. In fact, in high school we rarely ever hung out at her house. She preferred to stay at mine. My parents may annoy me, but I guess they're cooler than Lola's. Besides, I can never tell if Lola's parents like me or not. They sort of always give me the cold shoulder. Lola assures me that they're like that with everyone, but it still makes me uncomfortable.

Pushing her hair out of her eyes, Lola peers up at me from where she kneels on the ground in front of her suitcase. "Sorry. I know I've been rambling. How was it with your family?"

"It was okay." I carry an armload of shirts to my dresser.

"Want to switch families?" Lola jokes.

I shove the shirts in my middle drawer and bump it closed with my hip. "No thanks."

"That's what I thought." Lola scrunches her nose.

"Leo was kind of annoying though," I say, as I walk back to my suitcase which lays open on my bed.

"What's new?"

I chuckle. "Okay, I know he's always been a little irritating, but this was different. I got the feeling that he suspects I'm hiding something. It was like he was trying to goad it out of me all week."

Lola bites her lip. "Do you think your parents are suspicious?"

"No, they seemed clueless."

"Then I wouldn't worry about it. Besides, it's not like it will matter if you plan to drop the band anyway."

Scooping out my pants, I arrange them in my arms and head back to my dresser. They smell like my parents' laundry detergent. "I think I've decided to stay in it."

Lola lets out a tiny squeal. "Really? What made you change your mind? Did you hear from Beckett or something?"

My stomach twists at her words. "No, I didn't. But I like being in the band, and I don't want to quit." After putting away my pants, I lean my back against the dresser. Lola is still on the ground arranging her clothes by color or some nonsense like that. "And I'm really looking forward to this festival thing. Beckett thinks we might get discovered. Wouldn't that be wild?"

"You guys are awesome. It could totally happen."

I bite my lip, thinking. "But what if we are discovered? How will I explain it to my parents then?"

"Girl, if you guys get a recording contract, your parents will be thrilled."

"I know, but they'll also know that I lied to them."

"You didn't exactly lie. You just didn't tell them everything. There's a difference."

"Somehow I don't think they'll see it that way."

"Trust me, if you guys make it big your parents will overlook it."

I can't help but think Lola's projecting a little here. Sure, in the case of her parents that would be true. All they care about is success and money. My parents aren't like that. I take a deep breath to loosen up the knot in my chest. It doesn't matter what my parents think. I'm back in Seattle, and it's my life. I get to live it how I want.

"So, does this mean you're going back to rehearsal this Thursday?" Lola raises a brow.

I nod, my chest tightening. "Maybe things won't be so awkward between me and Beckett now that we've had some time apart." Even though I feel like I'm grasping at straws, I really hope I'm right. I know that I'm going to wait in agony all week to find out.

Only it turns out I don't have to wait that long. Thursday morning Beckett sends me a text asking if I'll come to rehearsal early. He wants to go over vocals before the rest of the band shows up. I know it's strictly professional, but my heart flips in my chest at the prospect of having some alone time with Beckett. If I had any hope that I was over him, the heart flippy thing confirms that I am not.

In fact, I'm so nervous when I pull up to his parents' house I think I might puke. Then I remember how sweet he was when I did puke at Ryker's party. My insides flutter at the recollection of him pulling my hair back from my face and rubbing my back. As I walk toward the garage, I wonder what Beckett I'll get today. Will it be the kind one who held my hair back at the party or the cold one from the coffee shop?

"Hey." Beckett looks up at me with a smile when I enter the garage. He's bent over his guitar amp, fiddling with some buttons.

I exhale lightly, my nerves settling a little. "Hi." Making my way to the keyboard, I set my purse down beside it and my sheet music on top.

"How was your Thanksgiving?" Beckett stands up and reaches for his guitar.

"Good. Yours?"

He shrugs. "It was okay."

"Did you come here?"

He nods, and I wring my hands in my lap, unsure of what else to say. Small talk always seems so awkward between the two of us.

"Wanna run through a few songs?" Beckett gets right down to business, and for once I'm relieved.

"Which ones?" I pick up my pile of papers.

"The two new ones first."

Rifling through the music, I find them and extract them from the stack. Then I flick on the keyboard.

"Actually," Beckett says. "I wanted to focus mostly on vocals, so I was hoping we would just use my guitar."

"Oh, okay." I flick the switch to off and rest my hands in my lap.

Beckett heads over to the corner of the garage and grabs two stools. "Why don't we both sit here?" He sets the stools next to each other. Then he climbs onto one, setting his guitar in his lap.

Pressing my lips together, I get up and walk with trembling legs over to the stools. As I sit down, I take a deep breath. I can smell Beckett's musky scent wash over me, and it causes my heart to race. Our knees are practically touching as he starts to strum his guitar, and my palms clam up. I wipe them on the thigh of my jeans and will my heart to slow down.

"I'll take the first verse and you take the second, okay?" He looks pointedly at me.

I nod, surprised. Usually I just sing back-up on this song. I wonder what made him change his mind about that. Not that it matters. I'm just grateful for the opportunity. When we get halfway through the song, the door leading into the house pops open. I see Beckett's shoulders tense, but he keeps playing, so I stay focused. Out of the corner of my eye I see the figure of a man standing off to the side watching. When I do dare a peek I notice that it's Tate. Beckett must realize this too, because he visibly relaxes.

Clapping rings out when we finish. Tate saunters over to us. "You guys sound great together. Like one of those folk duos."

"Thanks." I blush from his words.

Beckett's gaze slides over to me. "Yeah, I agree. I'm thinking of having us do an acoustic song together at the festival."

"You definitely should," Tate responds. "You two have a great vibe together."

Excitement bubbles inside of me at their

conversation. A song with just Beckett? It's like a dream come true. I fight hard to keep my expression neutral. I want to jump out of my chair and scream with delight.

Beckett rests his hands over his guitar. "So, what's the deal, Tate? You over here for dinner or something?"

Tate nods.

"Man, you spend more time here now than you did when you lived here."

Tate chuckles. "Times have changed, bro."

"I guess." Beckett grins, but I can tell it's forced.

Tate swings his arms to the side, clearly feeling the change in the atmosphere too. "Well, I'll let you two get back to it. Nice to you see you again, Star."

"You too, Tate."

As Tate makes his way back inside, he and Beckett share a look that I can't quite decipher. If only these Nash boys weren't so hard to read.

22

Beckett

Tate's right. There is something amazing about the way Star and I sound together. I've known it since the day she auditioned. At first it worried me, but now I'm thinking I can use it to my advantage. It may be the edge our band needs to be noticed at the festival. We already have the rock sound, and now we can add in something softer. By the time the guys arrive my head is swirling with the possibilities.

I share some of it with them, and they seem okay with it. Of course it's hard to tell lately. Ever since I got on them about Ryker's party they've been kind of short with me. Star seems to have relaxed around me tonight, but there's still some tension there. I guess we'll have to talk about our conversation at the coffee shop at some point. But I'm good with pushing that out for awhile. Right now I just want to get through the festival.

After the guys get all their stuff plugged in and ready, we start with *Can't Have*. As the band kicks it into high gear, I have a thought. I stop playing and speak into my microphone. "Hey guys, let's slow this one down a little too."

"But we're a rockband, man," Ryker groans. "It's bad enough that you want to do a couple of acoustic songs with Star, but now you want to slow down our other songs too?"

"What's wrong with changing things up a little?" I cock my eyebrow at him, challenging him to continue to question me.

"What if we don't want to change things up?" Ryker glances over at Pierce and Jimmy. "Do you guys want to change things up?"

Pierce shakes his head. Jimmy's eyes shift back and forth uncomfortably.

Irritation bubbles inside of me. "It doesn't matter what you guys think, okay? It's my band. I have the final say."

"Of course. Isn't that always the way?" Ryker shakes his head in disgust. "I'm so sick of having you dictate everything we do."

"I'm sorry, man, but that's the way it is," I say, my tone a little softer now.

"It doesn't have to be." Ryker peels off his guitar strap.

Warning bells go off in my head. "What do you mean?"

Ryker glances over at Jimmy and Pierce, giving them a subtle nod. "We're tired of your attitude, Beckett, and we're tired of your rules."

"Yeah," Pierce cuts in. "We're thinking maybe it's time we split up."

"What?" I feel like I've been sucker punched. "You can't do that."

"Oh, yes, we can," Ryker says.

I narrow my eyes at him, knowing there is one wrench in his plan. "But you don't have a lead singer."

Ryker's eyes rest on Star, and my stomach drops. Is she in on this? Of course she is. I should've known.

"So that's been your plan all along, huh? I thought it was weird how hard you pushed for her to join us." I rest my arms on my guitar, feeling suddenly weary.

Star stands up from the keyboard, throwing her arms up as if in surrender. "No way. You're not putting me in the middle of this drama. I'm not going to be used as some kind of pawn. I joined this band to work with all of you, and I'm not supporting this break up." Her gaze sweeps over all of us. "You guys need to work out your petty issues. When you do, you can give me a call." She scoops up her sheet music and purse, and then stalks out of the garage.

I watch her in awe. To me she's never looked more beautiful. On instinct, I take off after her. I catch up to her right before she gets in her car. "Star!"

She whips around, her hair lashing her in the face.

"Thanks for what you said in there."

Star shrugs. "I meant it. Clearly you guys have some issues to work out, but it's not worth breaking up the band over."

"You could've easily left with them. I know I haven't always been the easiest person to work with."

"You can say that again," she mutters under her breath.

I step forward. "Why didn't you?"

She bites her lip and I see the hesitation written on her face. "The truth is I joined the band because of you, and I have no desire to stay in it if you're gone."

Her words catch me off guard. The air around me shifts. All of the sudden I don't care about the consequences. I reach out and grasp Star's hand. "I need to go back in there and talk this out with them. But do you think maybe we could...grab a coffee or something after?"

Star's eyes widen, surprise evident on her face. "Sure. Just text me when you're finished."

I smile, and reluctantly drop her hand. It felt so good to hold it, almost like a lifeline. "See you soon," I say, before turning around and heading back to the garage. The guys are huddled together

190

in conversation when I enter. I can't lose them right before the festival. Besides, I'm anxious to see Star again. I know that it's on my shoulders to make this right, so I decide to take the higher road.

"Look, guys, I know I'm kind of intense most of the time."

"Kind of?" Ryker lifts his brows.

"Okay, so I'm really intense," I concede, and all the guys nod in agreement. "But it's just because I believe in our band so much. And the reason I do is because of you three. You're so talented. That's why I wanted you in my band. And I don't want to lose you guys." I take a deep breath, knowing the foreign words are going to be difficult to push from my throat. "So, I'm sorry."

Their stunned expressions tell me they weren't expecting it either.

"So are you saying that you'll back off a little?" Ryker asks.

I nod.

"Okay." Ryker steps forward and shakes my hand.

"You're all staying then?" I ask.

"It's not like we have a choice now." Ryker chuckles lightly. "Our plan sort of fell through."

I smile. "Yeah, you probably should've filled Star in beforehand."

Ryker locks eyes with me. "It wouldn't have made a difference. It seems she's not going to leave you, Beckett."

I swallow hard, knowing he's right.

When Star walks into the coffee shop she looks so hot in her skinny jeans and knee high boots. Her hair is swept back from her face in a loose ponytail, and her cheeks are flushed from the cold. When she sees me her face lights up, causing my heart to leap in my chest. This is all new to me, and my nerves are rattled. Yet, I don't want to run away. For once I want to stay here and see where it leads.

"Hey, Beckett." She slides into the seat across from me, her gaze landing on the two coffees on the table.

"Mocha, right?" I ask, hoping I didn't mess up.

She smiles. "How did you know?"

"I asked Ryker," I answer honestly. "He said that both you and Lola love mochas."

"He was right." She grins, looking pleased. "And that was sweet of you to ask him."

"Sweet, huh?" I wink. "Be careful. You're gonna ruin my image."

Star giggles, and it's as beautiful as her singing. "Don't worry. I won't tell anyone." She picks up the cup in front of her, and takes a tentative sip.

The coffee shop is pretty dead tonight. Only a few other patrons are scattered throughout. Most are on their laptops. I hear the clicking of keys from over my shoulder.

"Hey, thanks again for tonight," I say. "The guys and I worked things out after you left, and I owe it all to you."

"Me?"

"Yeah. They kind of didn't have a choice since they didn't have you as their lead singer."

She shakes her head. "I had no idea about any of it. I promise."

"I know." I take a swift drink of my latte.

"I'm glad it worked out. I was nervous about it."

"You were?"

"Yeah, I know I've only been in the band a short time, but I love it."

"I can tell." I curl my hand around my mug, working up the courage to ask her what I want to. Having conversations like this are hard for me. I'd rather hide behind my guitar. "Hey, when you said that you joined the band for me, what did you mean by that?"

"Oh." Her gaze drops to the table, her face flaming. "I just meant that I think you're super talented. Ever since the first time I heard you play I knew I would do anything to be a part of your band."

Disappointment sinks into my stomach at her words. I don't know why I expected her to say anything different. Every time she's confessed her feelings for me I've shot her down. Maybe I finally pushed her too far. Just because I finally decided to give her a shot, it didn't mean she would offer it to me.

"Beckett, what are we doing here?" Star asks.

"Isn't it obvious? We're having coffee." As if on cue, the espresso machine roars to life behind the counter.

"No, I mean, why now? Why tonight? You hardly say two words to me for weeks, and then today you want me to come early to practice. Then you ask me out for coffee. What gives?"

"I think I'd like to go back to when you were complimenting me and calling me sweet," I banter back, hoping to elicit a laugh or even just a slight smile. Instead, she presses her lips together and stares at me deadpan. "Okay, the truth is that I wanted you to come early to practice with me because…" I pause unsure of how honest I want to be. "I told you why. I want to do a couple of acoustic songs at the festival to give us an edge over the other bands. I know that Cold Fever will only do rock songs, there are a couple of other rock bands and I think a couple of country bands."

"So this is all just about the band?"

I want to say yes. Only that's not entirely true and at this point I feel like I owe Star the truth. "No, it's not." Leaning over, I prop my elbows up on the table. "I like you, Star. I have since the first moment I saw you. And I know I'm not great at showing it, but I'd like to change that."

"You would?" Star's face holds a skeptical look.

"Yeah, I would." I exhale, glad that's over with.

Star quietly takes a sip of her coffee. Then she sets the cup down and looks up at me with a serious look. "Beckett, I'm really sorry that I went behind your back to talk to Dante. I never should've done that."

"I get it. I know I haven't exactly been the easiest guy to talk to about things."

"Still. I feel bad." Star runs her fingertip over the rim of her mug, and I find myself imagining her fingers tracing my flesh. I shake my head and force my thoughts to cleaner subjects.

"I might have overreacted a little." I give her a lopsided smile.

"You? Overreact? No, not at all," she jokes.

"Yeah, you're right. It was completely justified." I smile to let her know I'm teasing.

She giggles again, and it's so cute I can't help myself. I reach across the table and place my hand over hers. "I'm not sure where to go from here."

"I find that hard to believe based on your track record with women."

"This is different, and this is new to me. Help me out here."

"Okay." Star sits up straighter. "Does this mean you want me to teach you to get close to people again?"

"Not people. Just you."

She smiles. "Well, you can start by asking me out on a date."

"A date, huh?"

"Yes, you know like when a guy takes a girl out for dinner or movie or something?"

"Ah, yes. I have heard of those." I chuckle. Then I sober up and look deeply into her dark brown eyes. "Would you like to go out with me?"

"When?"

"Saturday night?"

"I'd love to. Pick me up at seven."

"It's a date."

23
Star

"I still can't believe he asked you out on a date." Lola walks next to me as we make our way across campus. The early morning breeze kicks up her hair and it feathers against her pale skin. A few students walk in front of us, their heads down. To my right, I catch sight of a couple sitting on the grass bent over their textbooks. "Ryker said that's like a first for Beckett."

My insides coil into knots when I remember our conversation about the girl Dante stole from him. Again I wonder why everyone is so secretive about it. Clearly there had been another girl in Beckett's life. Why the charade?

"I know I've been kind of skeptical about Beckett," Lola says.

I turn my head to her and give her an incredulous look. "Kind of?"

"Okay, so I've been a lot skeptical, but I have to say that I think he really likes you. I mean, you've given him every reason to run away and yet he keeps coming back."

"Gee, thanks." We turn a corner, and the wind sprays over me causing me to shiver. I pull my jacket tighter around my body. It sure is colder here than back home.

"You know what I mean." Star nudges me in the side. "I'm just saying that maybe I was wrong about him."

"Yeah, he definitely surprised me last night." Warmth fills my insides when I recall how he touched my hand and looked into my eyes like he could see right through to my soul.

"So what are you going to wear?"

Leave it Lola to think about clothes. I sigh. "I hadn't even thought about it actually. I don't even know where he's taking me."

Lola links arms with me and grins devilishly. "It's fine. Leave the wardrobe selection to me."

I glance at Lola's black belted jacket, colorful scarf, jeans and knee high boots. Then I peer down at my oversized jacket zipped over my bulky sweater. "Okay, yeah, that might be good."

A group of students walk past us, going in the opposite direction. I catch a whiff of cologne that vaguely reminds me of Beckett. It causes my heart to skip a beat. I can't wait for tomorrow night. Picturing Beckett's perfect lips, I imagine how they'll feel against mine, and just the thought of it steals my breath away.

"Hello. Earth to Star." Lola's voice snaps me back into focus.

I inhale sharply and look at her.

"Whoa. Where'd you go?"

"Just thinking." I lower my gaze to the scuffed toe of my boots.

"Thinking about Beckett I bet." She winks, and my cheeks heat up.

When am I not thinking about Beckett?

Yesterday I couldn't wait for tonight to get here. But now that it is, I feel sick. My hands tremble as I button my pants, and it takes me several tries since my fingers are slick with moisture. I've never been this nervous before a date. Then again, I've never gone out with a guy like Beckett before. In fact, I never dreamed a guy like Beckett would ever ask me out. It's like a dream, really. Now let's just hope I don't make a total fool of myself tonight, so we can have a second date.

"Looking sexy," Lola coos. "I love that outfit on you."

"You are the one who picked it out," I remind her with a smile. Using my fingers, I smooth down my hair. Glancing at myself in the full length mirror we have on the door, I turn in circles to catch my reflection. Since Beckett assured me it was casual, I'm wearing jeans, boots, and a sheer flowing shirt. I have on my favorite earrings, and I borrowed one of Lola's necklaces. My heart hammers in my chest, and at first I don't even notice the knock on the door.

Lola gives me a funny look as she steps forward to answer it. As she opens the door, I swipe my hands down the thigh of my jeans. My breath hitches when I see Beckett standing in the doorway, wearing jeans and a white shirt that clings to his body and exposes almost the entirety of his arm tattoo. He smiles at me, and I force my legs to move forward even though it feels like I'm wading through mud.

"You look gorgeous," he says with a grin.

"Thanks," I say, as I reach for my purse.

Lola gives me a pointed look, and then gently shoves me out the door. "Okay, you two, have fun."

I stumble into the hallway as Lola slams the door behind us. "Sorry about her," I mumble. "She has control issues."

"Clearly." Beckett grabs my hand and threads his fingers through mine. "Ready?"

Biting my lip, I nod. He guides me out of the dorms and toward his truck. The parking lot is quiet, the night air still. Even though it's chilly outside, I feel like I'm burning up. Beckett's hand engulfing mine is sure distracting. With as much as I'm sweating, I feel bad for the guy. I hope he's not totally grossed out. When we reach his truck he releases my hand to open the door for me.

I raise my eyebrow. "Such a gentleman. Who knew?"

"Just wait." He winks as I slide into the car. My heart flutters in my chest as he goes around the truck to get in the driver's seat.

"Where are we going?" I ask, when he pulls out onto the street.

"You'll have to wait and see." He keeps his gaze trained on the road ahead.

"For a guy who doesn't date, you certainly seem sure of yourself," I joke. But really I'm fishing, hoping he'll let something slip.

"I'm always sure of myself."

I relax back in my seat, allowing some of the nervousness to wash away. Now that Beckett and I are bantering, everything seems normal - comfortable even. Sighing in satisfaction, I roll my head in Beckett's direction. I take in his profile in the darkness, as lights from other cars flicker over his skin. His muscular arms grip the steering wheel, and I imagine what they would feel like wrapped around me. My insides dance at the thought. Afraid he'll catch me staring, I turn my head toward the window. When we come upon a familiar street, my shoulders tighten. Flicking on his blinker, Beckett confirms my suspicion.

"You're taking me to your parents' house?"

"Don't worry. They're not home tonight. Tate took them to dinner."

"I feel like I'm back in high school. So are we, like, going to listen to music and make out in your room?" Once the words are out, I'm shocked by my own boldness.

"You wish." Beckett winks as he pulls into his parents' driveway. He cuts the engine, pulls his keys out of the ignition and looks at me. "There are some things I want to show you."

His face is close to mine, and my eyes lower to his lips. If only he'd just move forward a little. I want to kiss him so bad. But instead, he pulls away and opens the door. I swallow hard and hop out of the passenger side. Beckett swaggers toward me, tucking his hand into mine. Grateful for the affection, I smile at him as we walk toward the house. Beckett enters through the garage.

"Don't you have a key?" I ask.

"Don't need one. What I want to show you is in the garage."

I freeze. "Please don't tell me we're going to practice."

"Star." Beckett looks pointedly at me. "What kind of guy do you think I am? I asked you out on a date, and a date is what I'm going to give you."

"Okay." I smile. "Just making sure, because so far this is unlike any date I've ever been on."

"I'll take that as a compliment."

I chuckle at his smug attitude. Much to my chagrin, he drops my hand and walks up to a cabinet against the wall. He unhooks the cabinet and the doors swing open. "Remember that night we wrote together in my apartment?"

"How could I forget? It was the night you told me I was terrible at writing lyrics."

He runs a hand over his head. "It was also the night that I told you about my dad. Do you remember that, or do you only remember bad things?"

I smirk. "No, I remember that too."

"And it was the night that you told me I needed to learn how to be close to people."

"Ah, yes, the deal you broke," I remind him.

He waggles his fingers at me. "You really like to harp on the negative, don't you?" Stepping closer, he swipes a fingertip across my cheek. "It's a good thing you're so cute."

My body goes numb from his touch, and I lose the ability to speak.

"You were right. I'm not good at letting people in, Star, but you make me want to change. I want to open up to you." He reaches into the cabinet and pulls out an old guitar.

I'm a little confused, but wait for him to

continue.

"This was the first guitar I ever played." Beckett rolls it around in his fingers, a faraway look on his face. "My dad got it for me when I was just a little kid. Dad used to spend hours teaching me how to play. Those were some of the best times of my life."

"That's cool. Neither of my parents have a musical bone in their body. I actually taught myself how to play piano. I still don't think they completely understand my fascination with music."

Beckett nods. "I don't think my parents understand me anymore either."

"What changed?"

"A lot." A funny look crosses Beckett's face and then he sets down the guitar. Ignoring my question he pulls out some rolled up posters. He unrolls one of them and holds it up. The slick paper keeps trying to roll back up, so he has to keep pulling it tight. "These are posters I collected of my dad's band. Anytime I find one, I buy it."

I think of the other night at my dorm room when Beckett told me about why his dad quit the band. Resting my hand on his arm, I look into his eyes. "You're really proud of him, aren't you?"

"Yeah." He smiles, his eyes alight with excitement. "He got to live his dream, even if it was only for a little while."

"I'm sure you'll get the chance too," I assure him, my hand still resting on his arm. I'm so glad he hasn't shaken it off yet.

"I hope so." He whirls around to face the cabinet again, and my hand reluctantly slips from his arm. I wish the moment hadn't been broken, but I have to admit I am curious as to what he'll show me next. "Here is a picture of my very first performance." He flashes a photograph at me.

I snatch it from him, my gaze connecting with the glossy image. Laughing, I cover my mouth with my hand. "Look at your hair."

"My brother always wore his long. I was just trying to look like him." He grabs the picture from me.

"He still wears his long," I say.

"I know. He's had the same look for years. What can I say? He's stuck in the nineties."

"Yeah, that's like my mom. Only she's stuck in the eighties, I think. She still thinks big hair is in."

"If I'm like that I hope my kid'll knock some sense into me." Beckett puts the photograph back in the cabinet.

"I thought you didn't want kids," I say, remembering what he said the night of the party.

Beckett turns to me. "I didn't say that. I just said that I wouldn't give up my dream for a family."

"Isn't that the same thing?"

"I used to think so. Now I'm wondering if maybe there's a way to have both."

I want to ask him when this big epiphany came about, but I lose my courage. Instead, I peer behind him. "Anything else in there you want to show me?"

He rubs his stomach. "No. Now we go eat. Then I have somewhere else I want to take you."

"Sounds good to me." I hadn't even realized I was hungry, but now I find myself ravenous.

24
Beckett

After dinner I drive Star to a place I've never shared with anyone else. To a place I've never wanted to share with anyone else. I marvel at the fact that I even want to share it with Star. When I pull off the road and park in the middle of nowhere, I see the slight lift of Star's brows and it makes me want to laugh. I wonder what she's thinking inside the pretty little head of hers. All around us is a vast expanse of dried grass and big leafy trees. The street is quiet, and there isn't another car in sight.

"Somehow I thought you would take me somewhere a little nicer to have your way with me."

"You seem to be pretty obsessed with that idea. You must really want me." I nudge her gently in the side.

She rolls her eyes. "You're the one who brought me here."

"It's not what you think." I open the car

door. "C'mon."

The air has cooled down considerably, and Star shivers as we walk on the crunchy grass. I wrap my arm around her shoulders and pull her to me. Her hair falls against my arm, emitting a floral scent. Our feet clomp on the hard dirt and crackle over leaves. When we get to a large gnarled tree, I stop. Pointing with my fingers, I find the place where I carved my initials into the trunk.

"Does that stand for Beckett Nash?" Star squints her eyes as she reads the crude letters. "Should I be looking for a girl's initials somewhere?" Her eyes rove over the rest of the trunk.

"No. I didn't come here with a girl. I've actually never brought anyone here."

Star's gaze sweeps the desolate field. "Where is *here* exactly?"

"Sit down." I slide down the tree trunk until my butt hits the ground. Star plops down next to me, bringing her sweet intoxicating scent with her. "When I was in high school, Tate left home and took off on a tour with his band. A few months later he got a DUI. After that he sort of spiraled out of control. Pretty soon he was using drugs, and doing a bunch of stupid stuff that eventually got him kicked out of his band. My parents were really upset about it, and they decided that I should stop spending so much time on music and find

208

something else to focus on." I scratch the back of my neck. "I think they thought that music was the root of all of Tate's problems. So I used to sneak off and come here with my guitar. I'd sit right here at this tree and play. I also wrote songs. In fact, several of the songs we play I wrote sitting right here."

Star's hand finds mine. "Is Tate still using?"

"No, he's clean now."

"That's good." Star rests her head on my shoulder. "I guess that's why you're such a stickler for your no drinking or drugs rule with the band, huh?"

"That's part of it, yes." My stomach clenches when I think of the other reason. That's a story I'm not quite ready to share. "It's just that everyone in my family let something derail their chances of making it big in the music industry. And it's a shame too, because they were so talented."

"I'm sorry, Beckett." Star's fingertips trace the inside of my palm, and the motion drives me wild.

I clear my throat. "Nothing be sorry about."

"It's okay to admit that something upsets you, Beckett."

I shrug. "Well, that's enough of all of this

serious talk." I drop Star's hand and then stand up, wiping my hands on the back of my pants. "I don't think I've jabbered this much about my life to anyone ever. I think I'm dangerously close to breaking out in hives."

Star giggles that amazing giggle of hers while she stands up too. "Well, I appreciate you telling me." Then she narrows her eyes. "Why did you tell me, Beckett?"

"Because I wanted you to know."

"Why?"

"I care about you, Star." I move closer to her. "More than I should."

"You do?" She looks up at me with those crazy innocent eyes, and I crumble.

Reaching up, I gently run my fingertips along her chin. Then I cup her face with my hands and lean close until my lips are almost touching her cheek. She smells like honeysuckle. "Yes, I do. No matter how hard I've tried to fight it, I just can't help myself when it comes to you."

She inclines her head toward mine, her eyelids fluttering. My heart picks up speed, and I lower my face to hers. I want so badly to kiss her, but something stops me almost like there is an invisible wall between us. With a jolt, I back up.

Star's shoulders slump and she sighs. "I don't get it, Beckett. One minute you draw me in, and the next you shut me out. I can't keep doing this with you. Either you want to be with me or you don't."

I run a hand over my head. "It's not that simple."

"It is for me." She whirls away from me.

Desperation blooms in my chest. "Where are you going?"

"Back to the car. I want you to take me home," she calls over her shoulder.

"Star," I call after her, but she starts walking faster. I jog to catch up. "C'mon, don't be like this."

"Please just take home," her voice wavers.

It breaks me, and I can't take it anymore. I don't want to hurt her. Grabbing her arm, I spin her toward me. With swift movements, I wrap my arms around her and pull her close. "Damn it, I can't believe I'm doing this. I've never done this before."

"What?" she murmurs into my chest. "Hugged a girl?"

"No, I mean I've never chased anyone before. I've never had a problem with a girl walking away from me. But you, Star, you're different. You're worth running after." I brush her hair away from her face. Her head tilts up toward mine, her lips pursed. I swallow hard and move back a little.

Her face hardens, and she pushes me away.

"I'm worth running after, but you don't want to kiss me."

"Believe me. I want to kiss you."

She places a hand on her hip. "Then why don't you?"

I hesitate. "I'm scared."

"Why? I brush my teeth," she says with a slight smile, breaking through the tension.

"No, I'm not scared to kiss you. I'm just scared of what I'll feel when I do." I sigh, pressing my forehead against hers.

"Is it so bad to feel something, Beckett?" Her voice is soft, her breath sweet as it feathers over my skin.

Without thinking on it any further, I reach up and cradle the back of her head with my hand. I pick my forehead off of hers, my gaze traveling down to her lips. I curl my other hand around her waist and pull her hips toward mine. Then I press my lips to hers. I had every intention of starting off softly, but the minute my mouth touches hers desperation fills me. I force her lips open with my tongue and slide it inside her mouth. She tastes faintly of cherries or something equally sweet. Her arms come around my waist, her hands skimming up my back before stopping at my neck. Star's fingers dance along my flesh, causing chills to brush over my skin. I kiss her even more firmly, and a satisfied sound comes from the back of her throat. I rub my hand over her neck and tighten my hold on her waist. Her lips grind against mine, her tongue exploring my mouth with vigor. Every time I've kissed a girl before, it was just a precursor for something else. This is different. This means something else entirely.

When we finally part, Star's lips are swollen and red, her cheeks flushed. She's never looked more beautiful. "Wow," she breathes.

I press my nose to her temple and speak into her ear. "That was the first kiss to top all other first kisses."

"That wasn't your first kiss, Beckett."

"It was the first kiss I've had like that." I pull back, searching her eyes. "And after this, we'll have many more firsts."

"I have a feeling that you're all out of firsts."

"That's where you're wrong, Star. Very wrong."

25
Star

I wake up with a giant smile on my face. By how sore my cheeks are, I surmise that I must've been smiling while I slept. Not that I'm surprised. Last night was one of the best nights of my life. Reaching up, I run my fingertips over my lips remembering how it felt when Beckett's lips were on them. Kissing him was unlike anything I've experienced. My memory flies back to my first slobbery messy kiss with Spencer, and I wince. Beckett's kiss was perfect, even better than I imagined it would be. Everything about last night was like my wildest fantasy finally coming to life. I can hardly believe it really happened. I'm still grinning like a stupid idiot when I sit and stretch my arms.

"Someone woke up in a good mood," Lola croaks from her bed. Her hair is sticking up everywhere, and lines from her pillow are painted on her face. "I guess the date went well."

I nod, the smile still pasted on. I'm

214

beginning to wonder if it will ever go away.

"I tried to wait up for you so you could tell me all about it, but I ended up crashing." She lifts her brows. "You were out late. Please don't tell me you already slept with him."

"No." I shake my head. "But we did kiss."

"Oooh, how was it?"

"The best." My insides soar, but when the reality of the situation hits me I feel my high withering. Last night was amazing, but will it last? I mean, what's going to happen now? Will Beckett wake up this morning and regret opening up to me the way he did?

"What's going on? Your smile just totally went away."

"I was just thinking." I chew on my bottom lip.

"Are you having second thoughts about Beckett?"

I run my fingers over the covers that are bunched up to my waist. "Not at all. I'm just hoping it's the same for him."

"You're worried that he's going to go back to being cold and distant like before?"

I nod. "Am I just being paranoid?"

Lola sits up, brushing her unruly hair away from her face. She pushes her covers down and shrugs her shoulders. "I don't know. I mean, up to this point he's been all over the map."

My stomach knots. "Thanks. That was really helpful," I say sarcastically.

"Would you rather I lie to you?" Lola swings her legs off the bed and stands up.

"No, I guess not." I sigh, laying my head back down on my pillow. "I just hope we're wrong."

"Well, now's your time to find out."

"What?" I sit back up.

Lola tosses me my phone. "It looks like he's calling you."

I catch the cell in my hand, my heart pounding. "Hello," I answer.

"Good morning, Star." His incredibly sexy voice is even more raspy in the morning.

"G-good morning, Beckett."

"Sleep well?"

"Um...yeah I did." The smile is back.

Lola rolls her eyes, grabs her towel and toiletries bag and leaves the room, no doubt heading to the restroom.

"I didn't," he says.

"Why not?" I scoot back and rest my head against the wall.

"I couldn't stop thinking about you."

My stomach flips. "Really?"

"Yes, really. So, do you have any plans tonight?"

"No," I say, and then mentally chastise

myself for answering too quickly. Does that make me sound desperate?

"Good, because if you did I was going to tell you to cancel them."

"Why?"

"Because after last night, I'm not sure I can ever go a day without seeing you again."

"Well, you might sometimes have to survive a day without me. It's not like we're conjoined twins," I tease.

"Thank God. That would just be gross."

I giggle.

"Wanna go out tonight?" he asks.

"I'd love to."

"Great. I'll be by at six to pick you up."

"Sounds good." I throw off my covers and get up.

"Oh, and Star?"

"Yes?"

"This time it's not casual. Wear one of those sexy skirts I like."

"With the strappy sandals?"

"You better stop talking like that or I'm coming over right now," he growls.

"Promise?"

"You want me too?"

"No," I say quickly, and then scramble to fix it. "I mean, yes, I want you to, but I promised Lola I'd hang out with her today. We're going to breakfast and then doing a little shopping."

"You sure know how to ruin a moment," he says.

"Sorry. I'll see you tonight, Beckett." I hang up, the smile still lingering on my face.

By Thursday night's rehearsal I realize that Beckett has held to his statement of never going a day without seeing me. We've been out every night this week. He's taken me to dinner, to a movie, and one night we even just hung out at his house and talked. Okay, we may have made out a little too, but mostly we talked. Even so, I am excited when I pull up in front of his parent's house. I wonder if I'll ever get tired of spending time with him. I sure hope not.

I grab my sheet music and purse off the passenger seat and hop out of the car. After closing the driver's side door, I turn toward the house. That's when I'm hit with a moment of hesitation. Things have been so amazing with Beckett and me all week, but we've been alone. This will be the first time around other people. Will it be uncomfortable? Will Beckett slip back into the old Beckett, or will he be the same sweet guy he is when it's just us? I'm almost afraid to find out. I freeze, unable to move forward. The garage door opens with a loud rumble and I flinch.

"Star?" Beckett spots me. "Are you coming

in?"

I take a deep breath. I'm late like always so the other guys are already there. Before I can force my legs forward, Beckett swaggers toward me. I take a few steps until we meet. My heart is hammering in my chest, awaiting his first move.

"I was wondering where you were." He wraps his arm around my waist, and nuzzles my cheek with his nose. "I missed you."

I smile, inhaling his familiar scent. Bringing my arms up I hug him tightly. His mouth brushes over my cheek until it reaches my mouth. He kisses me tenderly, slowly, softly. My knees soften.

Pulling back, he looks into my eyes. "I hate to hold up the practice, but I knew I wouldn't be able to focus until I got that out of the way."

"Me neither." With his arm around my waist, we walk into the garage together. I can tell the other guys are surprised. The only one that seems slightly less stunned is Ryker, which makes sense because I'm sure Lola's filled him in on what's happening. Still they recover quickly and we get practice rolling. The festival is only a week away, so rehearsal runs a little long. We all know how much is riding on this, and we want to sound perfect. When Beckett and I sing together I marvel at how our chemistry has grown even more since the last time we practiced. I had been a little nervous that our spark would have dwindled since we got together. But no, it seems that the spark has grown into a full blown flame.

Everyone is exhausted by the time we finish. Ryker yawns, Pierce rolls his neck, and Jimmy shakes out his arms. However, Beckett appears to have all the energy in the world. "Okay, guys. Only one more practice until the festival. I can't wait." He rubs his palms together in anticipation. Then he unhooks his guitar, sets it on the stand and rushes toward me. Taking me in his arms, he says. "You sounded so amazing tonight." Lowering his lips to my ears, he adds, "And you looked so damn hot too."

"You too." I kiss his cheek.

He squeezes me tighter. "Where do you want to go tonight? You choose."

"It's late, Beckett. I should probably get home."

"What are you, eighty? It's not late."

"Not for you." I play with the collar of his shirt. "You can sleep until noon. I have class in the morning."

"Fine. Tomorrow night then?"

"I was already planning on it."

"And this time it's your turn."

"My turn for what?"

"C'mon, Star. I've shared a lot with you this week. Tomorrow night you take me somewhere."

He tucks his finger under my chin. "I want to learn more about you."

"Okay." I smile, knowing exactly where I'll take him.

It feels weird to be the one in control this time. For the past week Beckett has dictated where we went and when. Not that it bothered me. I kind of liked it. If we were back in my hometown there are so many places I could take him; so many memories I could share. In Seattle I'm not familiar with much, and I don't have any memories here. However, there is one thing I know a lot about, and it's something I can show him anywhere that has a sky. So I drive out to the same spot he took me on our first date.

When I pull over and cut the engine, he turns to me with his brows furrowed. "Don't tell me you used to come here and play music too. That would just be too weird."

I giggle. "No, I've only been in Seattle a couple of months and the first time I came here was with you. But it's the perfect location for me to show you something." I exit the car and head to the trunk. After popping it, I pull out a blanket and join Beckett. Hand in hand we walk forward. Only I don't take him as far as the tree. Instead, I stop when we get to the middle of the field. I drop the blanket on the ground and spread it out over the dirt and grass. "C'mon." I lay on my back, my hair splaying out around my face.

"What are we doing?" He asks as he plops down next to me.

"Just trust me, okay? Lay down on your back like me."

"Okay, but you better not try to take advantage of me," he jokes.

"Don't worry." I chuckle.

Beckett does as he's told.

I glance over at his face and smile. "Now look up in the sky and tell me what you see."

"Stars."

"Yeah, and the moon right over there." I point to the bright yellow crescent shining over the backdrop of night. "See the star closest to the moon? The brightest one in the sky? That's Sirius."

"Okay, well then I will take it seriously."

"Not serious," I say with a slight giggle under my words. "Sirius is what the star is called. When I was a little girl my dad used to take me out to a field near our house at night. He would point out all the stars to me and tell me their names. Man, I used to love those nights. I loved those times with my dad when it was just the two of us."

Beckett's hand closes over mine, his fingers tickling my flesh. "Do you miss him?"

"Sometimes, I guess. But I was ready to leave home. I like my life here."

"I'm glad because I like you being here." Beckett squeezes my hand.

His words warm my heart and cause a smile to break out on my face. I don't think I've ever smiled more in my life than I have over the past week. "That doesn't mean that my dad didn't want me to follow in his footsteps. I think he always hoped I would."

"How come you didn't?"

"It wasn't my passion. It was my dad's. I appreciated his love for it, but my heart always leaned towards music."

Out of the corner of my eye I see Beckett's face turn toward me. "What made you love music so much?"

"I don't know. I think when I was little I dreamed of being a pop star the same way every little girl does. But at some point I realized that I really did have musical talent. So when I was around ten I asked my parents for a keyboard for Christmas. I think they thought I was crazy, but they bought it anyway. I started playing around on it, and bought some books about playing keyboard." I shrug. "I guess it just came naturally to me."

"That's amazing. I still can't believe you taught yourself to play. That takes some real dedication."

I turn my head to look at him, our eyes locking. "I think when you feel strongly about something you'll do whatever it takes to see it through."

It's silent as we stare at each other. Usually silence bothers me, but in this moment as I stare into Beckett's eyes I feel that words would cheapen the moment. His fingers trace the inside of my palm, and he looks at me with an intensity I've never seen in anyone before. It's like we're communicating without saying anything. I can see in his eyes the turmoil that he's wrestling with. It's almost like I can see the demons that live behind his irises. But I can also see what he feels for me, and that is something I can cling to. After several minutes, the moment is broken when Beckett smiles at me and then turns his head back to look up into the sky.

26
Beckett

"Wanna know which star is my favorite?" I roll over, propping my elbow up on the blanket.

"Which one?" Star still stares up at the inky black sky.

"This one." I lean over her, swiping my finger across her cheek until it reaches her lips.

"Really?" She smiles up at me.

"Really." I nod, running my fingertip over her bottom lip. "And I'm tired of just staring at this Star."

"What do you have in mind?" She raises a brow.

"This." I bend over her, placing each arm around her head. Then I catch her lips in mine. Her hands come up around my face, drawing me closer. I press my lips hard against hers and coax her lips open with my tongue. Then I dart my tongue in her mouth and slide it against hers, tasting her sweetness. A tiny moan of pleasure escapes from her throat and it's beautiful, just like how she sings. It takes all my willpower to keep my arms in place, my body slightly elevated from hers. I know if I go any further I won't be able to stop myself. And this isn't how I plan to have our first time. I kiss her until I can't take it anymore. Then I push myself off and sit up, willing my body to stay calm.

She exhales and sits up too pushing her hair out of her face. Her cheeks are flushed, and her lips are swollen and red. A look of sheer desire passes over her features and she scoots toward me. I know I should back away, but I can't. She clamps her mouth over mine while her hands work their way under my shirt. Her fingertips slide across my chest, and they're so soft it feels like silk. When her hands move down toward my pants, I grab them in an effort to stop her. If she touches me, it'll be over. I only have so much self control.

"What?" She pulls away from me, searching my eyes. "Why did you stop me?"

"I told you. I want to take things slow."

"Don't you want me?" She sticks her bottom lip out in a pout.

"Of course. More than anything."

"Then what's the problem?" Her tone is hard, her eyes narrowed.

"I don't want our first time to be in the middle of a dirty field." I wink at her. "Believe me, I have big plans for us. Roses, scented candles, a bubble bath, the works." Her lips start to quiver, and I see moisture in her eyes. "Hey." I reach up and graze her cheek with my hand. "What's going on with you? Why does this bother you so much?"

She stares at me for a minute, biting her lip. Then slowly she opens her mouth. "Do you want to know why Lola is so protective of me? It's because she thinks I need someone to take care of me. Like without her I would have no social life at all. And I guess she's kind of right. I was homeschooled up until freshman year. I begged my parents to let me go to high school, and they reluctantly agreed. I met Lola at the first party I ever went to freshman year. It was supposed to be a date. I had a huge crush on this boy named Jared from my math class. He asked if I wanted to hang out one Saturday night and I said yes. He ended up taking me to a party. I didn't drink, but he did and pretty soon he was all over me. I got scared. I'd never even kissed a boy before. I didn't want to go any further but he kept pushing himself on me. Lola was there and saw the whole thing. She intervened and got Jared to leave me alone. Ever since then she's made it her goal in life to help me."

"Okay." I grab her hand and weave her fingers through mine. "I still don't get what this has to do with me."

"I've only gone out with two boys my entire life – Jared and Spencer. Jared wanted nothing to do with me after that party. He spread a rumor around school about me being nothing but a tease. Then Spencer and I went out for two years, but he ended up cheating on me because I wouldn't have sex with him. He said that guys have needs and he had to satisfy that somewhere."

Now I get it. "Those guys were idiots. Trust me. I've been with a lot of girls."

"I know, and that's why—"

"No, let me finish," I silence her. "I'm not proud of that fact, believe me. Now that I've met you I wish I hadn't used girls the way I did. But you know what, Star? Those girls aren't the ones I'm with right now. I'm here with you. And I don't want you to have sex with me because you're afraid if you don't I'll leave you. That's not how it is with us." I lean in and kiss her softly on the lips. "I want you to see yourself the way I see you."

"What do you mean?"

"You don't give yourself enough credit. You always think you have to prove yourself, but you don't. You're the most amazing person I've ever met. I wish you could see that."

She smiles. "You really think I'm amazing?"

"Figures that's the part you'd cling to." I

curl my lips upward.

"I think you're pretty amazing too."

"Well, who doesn't?" I tease, nudging her.

"At least you're humble about it." She grins.

"So, what do you say? Can we do this my way now?" I ask her.

She nods. "Yeah. Besides, I can't wait for the roses and scented candles. Who knew you were such a romantic?"

I lean into her, brushing my lips against her skin. "I can't wait to show you just how romantic I can be."

It's been two weeks since Star and I started dating, and I feel more comfortable with her than I've ever felt with anyone in my life. Ryker always teased me that one day I'd meet someone who would reform me, but I always told him he was crazy. I never thought a girl could change me like this. But then again, I've never met anyone like Star before.

"So tell me." Star leans into me, bumping her cheek on my shoulder. It's Friday night and we're hanging at my apartment, lounging on my couch and eating Chinese takeout. "What should I expect tomorrow?"

I kiss her swiftly on the mouth. "You should

expect to be the hottest chick at the festival."

She giggles against my lips. "Well, of course. But other than that?"

I sit back against the couch cushions. "It's gonna be rockin'. There will be a lot of bands, music playing all day, food vendors out, people everywhere."

"Do a lot of people come?" Star's face pales.

I grasp her hand. "You don't need to be nervous. You're gonna be great, trust me."

"You sound like Lola."

"I knew there had to be something good about her," I say sourly.

"C'mon, she's not that bad."

"She acts like she's your freaking bodyguard or something."

"I explained that."

"Still. You're both grown-ups now. She needs to back off a little," I say.

Star bites her lip. "I know. I've been meaning to talk to her about it."

"You said yourself that you're not that shy girl you were in high school." I bend toward her. "And I can vouch for that. You're one of the bravest girls I know."

"Oh, stop." She waves my words away.

"You are. I know you can't see that, but I can." I touch her face. "Think about how you stood up to the band a couple weeks ago. Not to mention all the times you put me in my place."

"That's different. I'm comfortable with you guys."

"You haven't always been." I tip her face to look at me. "And you sing in front of crowds of people all the time. You're braver than you give yourself credit for."

"I hope that's true tomorrow."

"It will be. I believe in you."

I brush my lips against hers, softly. She moans and then presses her mouth firmly to mine, her tongue licking across my bottom lip. Growling against her mouth, I grab her around the waist and crush her to me. I stick my tongue into her mouth and swirl it around, tasting her. My fingers tangle in her hair, while hers rake up my back. I hear the door pop open from over my shoulder.

"Whoa, sorry," Tate's voice rings out.

I push away from Star and peer up at Tate. "Hey, man. Next time knock."

"I'm not knocking before walking into my own apartment," Tate counters, closing the door behind him. "You have your own room, you know?"

"Maybe Star and I like the couch better." I raise my eyebrow.

Tate just laughs as he makes his way over to the recliner and plops down into it. "Hey, Star."

He nods in her direction. "How do you put up with this guy?"

"He's not so bad." Star nudges me.

"Not so bad. I thought you said I was amazing." I wink at her.

Her cheeks flush, and her gaze drops to her hands. "Well, it's getting late. I better take off." She glances up at me. "See you tomorrow?"

"I'll pick you up bright and early." I follow her to the door.

She looks over at Tate. "G'night, Tate."

"Night, Star."

I kiss her softly on the lips, and then open the door.

"See you in the morning." She gives me a slight wave of her hand.

"I can't wait." After watching her walk down the hall for a minute I close the door and walk back inside.

Tate whistles at me. "Never thought I'd see the day."

"What?" I feign confusion.

"You are totally whipped."

"No, I'm not." I sink down on the couch.

"Believe me, you are."

"I just like her, that's all."

"I can see that." Tate smiles. "And I'm happy for you, bro."

"Yeah, me too." I smile back.

This morning Star is wearing one of those skirts that drive me crazy. As we unload our stuff out of the truck, I can't help but stare at her butt. A couple of times she catches me and her face reddens. It's so cute, I want to just shove her back in the car and forget the whole performance. But I don't act on it. That's not how things are going to happen between Star and me. She means too much to me for us to have our first time in my truck.

I spot Ryker pulling into the parking lot with Jimmy and Pierce in tow. After they park, I wave in their direction. Then I plant a quick kiss on Star's cheek. "The gang's all here, baby. Are you ready?"

She gives me a nervous look, her gaze scouring the area. "I think." I can see her eyes widen as she takes in the giant stage set up outside, the huge crowd of people already gathering, and the food vendors scattered throughout. It is definitely going to be the biggest show we've played with her.

"Star, trust me. You're gonna be amazing like always."

"Thanks."

"Anytime." I pick up my guitar case. "Now, let's go get the guys and get ready."

"You go ahead. I'm gonna use the restroom

really quick and then I'll meet up with you."

I curl up my nose. "I think they just have port-a-potties here."

She gives me a rueful look. "When you gotta go, you gotta go."

"True." Before she can walk away, I grab her arm. "Hey, you okay?"

"Fine. I'll see you in a minute." She forces a smile and scurries off.

I watch her leave, a funny feeling in the pit of my stomach. She's more nervous than I've ever seen her. I hope she's going to be fine. Still worried, I carry my guitar case and head over to Ryker's van.

When I get there, Ryker pulls me aside while Pierce and Jimmy work on pulling out their equipment. "Hey, man, I've been meaning to talk with you."

"Yeah?" I lean against the side of the van, my leg bent. "About what?" I'm hoping this isn't going to be another conversation about the band breaking up.

"About Star."

I cock my head to the side. "What about her?"

Ryker shoves his fingers into the pocket of his jeans. "Are you serious about her, man?"

"Yeah, I am."

"It's just that Lola says Star's pretty into

you, you know? So I wanted to make sure that you weren't just using her or something."

"No, man, not at all." I run a hand over my head. "I really like her. More than I thought possible, actually."

"Yeah, I kind of thought this might happen."

"What do you mean?" I'm surprised by his words.

"I could tell you liked her the minute I introduced you two. I think that's why I pushed so hard for her to be in the band."

"I thought it was because you wanted her," I tell him.

Ryker shrugs. "Not gonna lie, when I first saw her at open mic night I thought she was pretty hot. But then I met Lola and I knew right away that she was the one I wanted to be with. Besides, I saw the way Star looked at you that night."

"Really?" I didn't notice Star that night, but it makes me happy to realize that she noticed me.

"Yeah, and I just kept thinking that if you gave her a chance maybe she'd be the girl to soften you." He punches me good-naturedly in the upper arm. "I can see that I was right."

"It seems like you were." I glance back toward the restrooms and wonder what's taking Star so long. "Speaking of which, I better go check on her. She was pretty nervous when we got here."

"It is a little overwhelming," Ryker agrees.

"Yeah, you're right." My stomach tightens as my gaze sweeps the chaos around us.

27
Star

"Hey," a voice calls to me when I leave the restroom. A band is already on stage and the music pulsates under my feet.

I whirl around and come face to face with Dante. My pulse quickens, and I wonder what he wants. My gaze sweeps the area. There are a few people heading to the restrooms, some with kids in tow. In the distance I see the band playing on stage, and the crowd of people dancing out in the middle of the field. Others are standing in food lines or sitting on the grass. When I don't see Beckett, I heave a sigh of relief. The last person I want him to see me with is Dante. "What?" I cross my arms over my chest. I know I should just run away, but I'm curious why he stopped me in the first place.

He smiles, noticing my defensive stance. "I take it Beckett's told you about me."

"Maybe," I respond coyly.

"Don't believe a word of it. He's just

bitter." He steps closer to me, and I back up. "You don't have to be scared. I'm not going to bite. I just wanted to wish you good luck."

"Thanks," I say quickly, and start to turn away. I need to get back to Beckett before he starts wonder-ing where I am.

"So are you and Beckett together now?"

My shoulders stiffen. "Not that it's any of your business, but yes."

"What the hell do you think you're doing?" Beckett's voice startles me, causing me to flinch. I spin around to see him stalking in Dante's direction. His hands are balled into fists at his sides, and his jaw is clenched. I've never seen him look so furious, and that's saying something.

Dante flashes him a sickening grin. "Just having a conversation with the lovely lady."

Beckett rushes him, and shoves him against the port-a-potty. "How dare you. You stay away from her."

"Beckett." I run to him, placing a steadying hand on his arm. "It's okay. Nothing happened. Come on."

"Just stay back, Star," Beckett commands, harshly. Shocked, I slink back. "Dante, if I ever see you talking to Star again, I swear to God I'll kill you." Beckett throws him back and turns away. He grabs me by the hand and pulls me forward. Hesitantly I follow his lead. My heels click on the pavement with each hurried step.

"What was that all about?" I ask.

"Nothing." He keeps his gaze trained in front of him.

I stop walking and jerk my arm out of his grasp. "That was not nothing."

Beckett glances over to where he left Dante. I look too, but Dante is nowhere in sight. "What did he say to you?"

I shrug. "He just wished me good luck for today."

"Did he hit on you?"

"No." I shake my head. "Is that what this is about?"

"I don't want you talking to him again, okay?"

"Why not?"

"Seriously. Are you trying to piss me off?" Beckett glares at me. "Because I said so."

A bitter laugh escapes through my lips. "Are you serious? That's the reason? Because you said so? We may be dating, but that doesn't mean you get to run my life."

"Star." He circles his hand around my wrist. "Please."

I soften under his touch, but I'm not ready to let him off the hook that easy. I need him to be honest with me. "Tell me why."

Beckett drops my arm and groans. "God,

you are so infuriating sometimes."

"Oh, and you're not?" I cock an eyebrow. "You practically beat up a guy for merely talking to me. Then you demand that I never talk to him again, but you won't tell me the reason."

"Damn it, why can't you just trust me? The guy is bad news, so stay away from him."

"I'm sure that's true, Beckett, but I want to know what happened between the two of you. Why can't you be open with me about it?"

He grabs me by the shoulders, and the sudden movement shocks me. "Star, just promise me!"

Unnerved, I shove him backward. "What the hell is wrong with you?"

"I don't want to lose you like I did Quinn," he says in a rush of words.

I freeze. "What?"

Beckett exhales slowly. "I've only known you a short time but I really care about you, and I've opened up to you more than anyone else. The thought of losing you now scares the shit out of me."

"You're not going to lose me, Beckett." I reach my hand out and gently touch his arm. "Is Quinn the name of the girl Dante stole from you?"

Beckett nods.

I run my fingers down his forearm until they reach his hand, then I thread my fingers through his. "That's not going to happen with me. I'll never cheat on you with anyone, especially not Dante. I only want you."

Beckett gives me a funny look. "Is that what you think? That Quinn was my girlfriend?"

His words confuse me. "Wasn't she?"

Beckett slumps his shoulders, a shaky breath escaping from his mouth. "I don't think I can do this."

My stomach tightens. "Do what?"

"Talk to you about Quinn."

I feel sick. *What is it about this girl?* "Please?"

"It's too hard to talk about. Can't you just trust me on this?" Beckett leans into me, brushing his lips against my cheek. My knees buckle. I want to nod in agreement, but I can't. For some reason I can't let this go. I don't want there to be anymore secrets between us.

"I do trust you, Beckett, and now I need you to trust me. You can tell me anything, and it won't change the way I feel for you."

"I never should've mentioned Quinn to you. I'm sorry, Star."

"Don't be. Just tell me about her."

"I can't." He shakes his head.

"You said you cared about me. When you care about someone you don't shut them out."

"You're right. It's just that I've never talked

about this with anyone outside of my family and Ryker."

"Didn't you say we'd have many firsts together?" I smile in an effort to lighten the mood.

"I did, didn't I?" Beckett grins back, and it lights up his whole face. He touches my cheek lightly with the palm of his hand. "I can't believe I'm going to do this, but I guess you do deserve an explanation for how I've been acting." His hand falls away from my face, and he takes a deep breath. "Quinn's my sister."

It feels like the ground flies out from underneath me. I hold tightly to Beckett to keep from falling over. "I didn't know you had a sister. I thought Tate was your only sibling."

Beckett swallows hard, his gaze scouring the area around us. People are milling about. "Can we go somewhere else to talk about this?"

"Do we have time right now?" By the distressed look on his face I kind of feel bad for pushing him to tell me today.

"Yeah. Our set isn't for a few hours."

I nod, my curiosity winning out. "Okay."

Beckett leads me to his truck. Once we are both inside he turns to me, his face a mask of despair. My chest tightens, and I know that whatever he's going to say it's going to be bad. I only hope it doesn't ruin things between us. It should make me feel relieved that Quinn is his sister, not an ex-girlfriend, but for some reason it doesn't. It only widens the distance between us, because the fact that he has another sibling is a huge thing to have hidden from me. Snatching up my hand, he places it in his lap. Absently he strokes my flesh with his fingertips. I stay silent, waiting for him to speak.

When he does, it's so soft I have to hone in to hear it. "I know I was kind of an ass when we first met."

I'm a little taken aback. It's not how I expected him to start this conversation. I have no idea what our meeting has to do with his sister, but I keep quiet and listen.

"The truth is that when I saw you, the only thing I could think of was how much you look like Quinn." He keeps his eyes lowered, staring at my hand in his lap. "You have the same brown hair and eyes, a similar build. But it's more than that. You're innocent like her, sweet like her, talented like her."

I smile at that. "If you love her so much, why would you hate that I'm like her?"

"Because it's painful for me to think about her, and I didn't want a constant reminder around me all the time." He lifts his eyes to mine. "And because I failed her, and I didn't want to fail you."

Seeing the sadness in his eyes breaks me open. "What happened, Beckett?"

"Quinn was born two years after me, and she was like my little shadow. I kind of hated it. When I started the band she begged me to let her join. Of course I said no. Who wants their kid sister in their band? That wouldn't be cool. But Quinn was stubborn, and when she wanted something she did whatever it took to get it. At one of my shows she met Dante. He allowed her to join his band, and pretty soon they hooked up." His face hardens. "Dante's a drug addict, and my sister started using with him. I tried to get her to stop, tried to get her to break it off with Dante. When that didn't work, I went after Dante. I threatened to kill him if he didn't leave my sister alone." He shakes his head.

I reach out with my free hand and gently rub his arm. "Of course you did. You were trying to protect your sister."

"That's just it. I didn't protect her. She found out about me going to Dante and she got so angry. She refused to speak to me again." Anger darkens his eyes. "She died of a drug overdose less than a month later."

I gasp, my hand flying to my mouth. "Oh, Beckett. I'm so sorry."

He waves away my words. "I should've been there for her."

"Beckett, none of this is your fault. She made her own choices."

"She never should've been in this business, and she wouldn't have if it weren't for me."

I palm the side of his face and force him to look at me. "You can't put this on you. Your sister had a mind of her own. Just like I do. Just like you do. No one can make you quit playing, right?"

"I guess that's true." Beckett nods. "I just wish I could change things. Maybe if I had let her be in my band, or if she'd never been at my show. I don't know."

"You can't torture yourself with what-if's, Beckett."

"It's just hard not to." He locks eyes with mine. "Dante killed my sister, Star, and there's nothing I can do about it. I've tried everything. I even went to the police, but Quinn did those drugs willingly so they can't pin it on Dante."

"Now I totally get why you hate him so much." I squeeze his hand. "And I promise I'll never speak to him again. But, Beckett, you can't spend all your time worrying about me. I'm not going to make the same mistakes as Quinn. And I'm not going to hurt you."

"This is so hard for me."

"What is?" I whisper.

"Being with you like this. It was so much easier for me to have superficial relationships. I didn't ever have to worry about getting hurt or losing someone again. Now that I've let you in,

I'm terrified."

"I know, Beckett. If it helps at all, I'm scared too." A slight smile touches my lips. "But I think it's worth it."

"I hope so." The pain in his face cuts to my heart.

I lean forward and press my lips to his. "It is. Trust me."

28

Beckett

I feel lighter after talking to Star. The hard knot that always sits in the center of my chest seems to have loosened. The pain of Quinn's death still lingers in my heart. I know it will never leave. That saying about time healing all wounds is bull in my opinion. The pain will never go away, but at least I don't have to carry it alone anymore. When Quinn died, my family all grieved in separate ways. Mom retreated into her own world, Dad got angry with me, with Tate, with music. Tate was the only one who turned it into something good. It was the catalyst that helped him get clean and sober. I just pulled away from them all. It was easier that way. But as I walk through the crowds of people with Star's hand tucked in mine, I realize that I finally have someone to support me. I thought once I opened up to someone like this it would be like they owned a piece of me that I could never get back. Instead, I feel I've been given an incredible gift.

"Are you okay?" Star's voice is soft beside me.

"I am now."

"Are you ready to perform?"

"When am I not?" I wink.

"It's just that I feel a little guilty about forcing you to share all of that with me today. I mean, you should be focusing on your music." She glances over at me, her face ravaged with shame. "I'm sorry I was so selfish."

"Hey." I draw her to me. "You didn't make me do anything. Besides, I'm glad I told you. And I'm glad it was today."

"Really?" She peers up at me through her dark fringe.

"Yes, really." I kiss her on the forehead. "Now let's go find the guys. We're up soon." I lead her through the crowd of people, bodies gyrating as they dance. Country music drifts from the stage. When I look up at the band's name, I realize that we still have one band up before us. Grabbing Star by the hand, I lean in and press my mouth to her temple. "Dance with me, Star?"

She raises her brows in a question.

"We have time," I whisper loudly into her ear to be heard above the noise.

Star nods with a sweet smile. I wrap my arms around her waist and draw her to me. It's not a slow song, but I don't care. I want to feel her in my arms. Her hips sway back and forth, her waist pressing against me every once in awhile. Her hair billows around her face with each sensual move.

I lean into her. "Have I ever told you how sexy you are when you dance?"

Star's face turns crimson, and she shakes her head.

"Well, you are. Why do you think nature boy and all his friends never miss a show?"

"You mean Forrest?" Star laughs.

"Hey." I run my lips over her cheek. "Don't make me jealous."

"There's nobody you need to be jealous of, Beckett." Her words tickle my ear. "Trust me."

I trail kisses down her neck and relish the little gasps that emit from her throat. All around us couples dance and jump around. No one even notices us, and so I take advantage of the moment, pulling her tighter against me and running my lips up to her mouth. Covering her mouth with mine, I frame her face with both hands. Her fingers dance over my chest as she opens her lips to allow me inside. My tongue slides against hers, my hands caressing the soft skin on her face. I want to stay here forever, and never release her. My head swirls, and I feel a pang of disappointment as the song comes to a close. I draw back and look into her brown eyes. She smiles lazily at me, her heart shaped lips curling upward and the skin around her eyes crinkling. I marvel at how I could stare at her face forever and never get tired of it. I've never met another girl like her, that's for sure.

A louder faster song starts, and the guy dancing closest to Star bumps into her. She staggers to the side. I hold out my arm to steady her, but my arm gets knocked away by someone's back. Luckily Star regains her balance and doesn't fall over. The scent of overpowering perfume washes over me, and before I can register what's happening a girl's arm snakes around my waist.

"Hey, Beckett. I was hoping you'd be here," a low, raspy voice greets me.

I try to maneuver out of the girl's grasp, but she only grips me tighter. Swallowing hard, I look around for Star. This is just the kind of thing that will piss her off, I know it. Ever since we started dating I've worked really hard at ignoring my fan club. I don't even dare a peek at them after our shows.

"Where are you going? You certainly weren't this eager to get away last time."

Taking a deep breath, I glance up at the girl. I vaguely recognize her, but I don't remember her name. Shame washes over me at the realization. Star really does deserve someone better than a guy who has spent the last several years using up women. Speaking of Star, where is she? When I once again can't find her, my stomach drops. I imagine her taking in this whole scene and running off. Not that I blame her.

I shove the girl back. "Look, I'm here with someone."

"You're always with someone, baby. I know that. It doesn't bother me." The girl purses her over made-up lips at me.

"No, I mean I'm here with my—"

"He's here with his girlfriend," Star's voice booms from over my shoulder. Her fingers lace through mine, and relief washes over me.

"Girlfriend?" The girl laughs. "Beckett doesn't have girlfriends."

I step away from the girl and look at Star. "That's because I'd never met Star before. Now I have a girlfriend." Nuzzling into her cheek, I speak into her ear. "And she's the only girl I want."

Star nestles into me as the member of my former fan club stalks away.

"I'm sorry about that," I say.

Star just waves away my words. "I knew what I was getting into when we started dating. It's not your fault."

I wish I could agree with her, but that's not entirely true. If only I'd always been the type of guy that Star could be proud of. But if there's anything I've learned in this life it's that you can't change the past. So, I vow to myself that I will be a better man in the future. That I will be worthy of Star; that I won't let her down.

When the announcer calls our name, I give Star's hand an encouraging squeeze and then head to my microphone. After strapping on my guitar my gaze sweeps the crowd. I wonder if there are any producers or agents out there. My insides dance at the mere prospect. The drums start pounding behind me, so I reach down and strum my guitar. We play several of our fast songs and the crowd seems to like it. The sea of bodies gyrate and jump in sync just under our feet.

Turning to Star, I nod my head. Then I speak into the microphone. "Now we're gonna bring it down for a minute."

Star comes to stand beside me. I pull the mic off the stand and hand it to her. I can tell she's nervous, but she gives me a brave smile.

"You're going to be amazing," I whisper in her ear before starting the song.

A flush creeps across her face and she brings the microphone to her glossy lips. When her voice sings out, an involuntary smile spreads across my face. Sometimes I forget how good she is, and then she reminds me. My favorite part of the song is the chorus when we sing together. With the microphone between us, I stare into her eyes and sing.

> *Pretty smile, innocent eyes,*
> *Open and honest, not a disguise.*
> *Scarred and bruised, innocence stolen,*
> *Ripped away, my heart is broken.*

I catch the slight moisture in Star's eyes as she takes in the lyrics. The song has new meaning now that she knows the story. It has new meaning to me too. I give her a sad smile, savoring the connection and understanding between us. Star's hand reaches out and brushes my arm. Her touch gives me strength, and it reminds me that telling her was the right thing to do. The song comes to a close, but I don't feel like it's over. I feel like everything in my life is just beginning.

29
Star

"I can't believe this is our last night together for two whole weeks." Beckett pulls me into his lap, wrapping his arms around my waist. The credits from the movie we just watched are playing in the background, and popcorn kernels litter Beckett's coffee table.

"Sort of shoots down your whole 'never going a day without seeing me' idea, huh?"

"Well, it was an impossible dream." He rests his chin on my shoulder.

"I could stay here and not go home for Christmas break."

"Yeah, that'd be a great way to make your parents hate me already."

"Good point." My stomach clenches. I am not looking forward to telling my parents about Beckett, but I know I have to. "I wish I could take you with me, but I won't subject you to two whole weeks with my wacky family. You'd break up with me for sure."

Beckett steals a quick kiss on my neck, and a flush of desire runs through me. "I doubt that. I'm sure they're as amazing as you are."

I giggle. "No, I'm the only amazing one in my family."

"I see my humility is rubbing off on you." He nuzzles his nose into my cheek.

"Yeah, it must be," I banter back. "What about you? Are you going to your parents' for Christmas?"

He nods, his chin rubbing against my shoulder. "I think it will be good for us all to be together."

I run my fingertips over his rough hands, tracing the lines in his flesh. "It will be hard, won't it?"

"It always is." The rawness in his voice causes emotion to well up in my throat. I swallow it down.

"Do you have a picture of Quinn? I'd love to see what she looked like."

Beckett nods, and I slide off of his lap so he can get up. When he leaves the room I stretch my legs out on the couch and lean my back against the armrest. Sometimes it's hard to believe that Beckett and I have only been dating for a short time. I feel so comfortable around him, yet he still makes my heart race and my palms clam up. He has the ability to make my head spin in his presence, and I wonder if it will ever change. I certainly never felt this way with Spencer.

When Beckett returns he has a photograph in his hand. I bring my legs up to my body as he sits beside me. My bare toes brush over his jeans. "This was taken a couple of years ago." He drops the picture into my hand.

I lower my gaze, my eyes connecting with the glossy photo. "She's so pretty." Glancing up at him, I smile. "She looks a lot like you."

"And you." Beckett tucks his finger under my chin.

"Not really. We just have the same coloring."

"It's more than that." Beckett takes the picture back and stares at it, a wistful expression cloaking his face. "Quinn was the sweetest person I knew. There was an innocence and openness in her eyes that's just like what I see in yours."

"So what you're saying is that we're both naïve?"

"I wouldn't say naïve. I would say that you aren't jaded."

"Not yet anyway." I smile a little sadly, knowing that at some point Quinn had to have been tainted in order to take the path she did.

"You never will be if I have anything to say about it." Beckett turns to me and kisses me softly on the cheek. Then he drops the picture on the

256

coffee table. "Hey, I have something I want to talk to you about."

"Okay." I face him.

"I've been thinking about how awesome it was when we did those songs together at the festival."

"It was." A smile leaps to my face at the memory.

"I think we really have something together, Star." Beckett reaches for my hand, rolls it between his fingers. "How would you like to be the lead singer of our band?"

"What?" I'm dumbfounded. "No, it's your band."

"I don't mean instead of me. I mean with me. I don't want you to just sing backup anymore. I really think we can get a recording contract if we present ourselves as a team – you and me together."

My heart leaps in my chest. "I would love that."

"Me too." Beckett scoots forward, his head tilting toward mine. His hands come up around my face, and he crushes his lips to mine. I reach my arm out tracing my fingers up his neck and rest them behind his head. As I drink in the taste and feel of him, I know this is exactly where I belong.

"So, are you ever going to tell me about this new boyfriend of yours?" Mom stands at the stove, stirring a pot of noodles. Her brown hair frames her face in tiny curls, and an apron is tied loosely around her waist.

I sit at the barstool, my elbows propped up on the tile counter. "What makes you think I have a boyfriend?"

Mom swivels her head and smiles at me. "Oh, I don't know. Maybe that huge grin on your face and the fact that you get a text every few seconds."

As if on cue, my cell vibrates. I glance down at it.

Writing a song. Thinking about how much your lyrics suck.

I have to bite my tongue to keep myself from laughing out loud. I quickly type back. **Start being a jerk again, and I'll write another tortured song.** When I look back up Mom is staring at me wearing an amused expression. "Sorry. I didn't realize I was being so obvious."

"We sort of suspected it over Thanksgiving. Well, at least Leo did." She wipes her hands on a rag.

"He's pretty perceptive for a seventeen-year-old boy."

"He just looks up to you. He always has."

I think about Beckett and Quinn, and my

heart aches for all he's lost. Now I know why he's so sad. My life has been a walk in the park compared to his. Remembering how much he hated my cheery lyrics that first time we wrote together, I totally understand why now. Only now he makes me so happy that I can only write sappy lyrics again. I know, because right before I left to come here we tried to write together again. I grin, thinking about how he teased me endlessly that night. He said that he's ruined me and I'll never write a good song again.

My cell buzzes again. **Not gonna happen.**

Which part? You being a jerk, or me writing a tortured song?

Both.

Mom leans across the counter toward me. "So tell me all about him. I want to know everything."

I squirm uncomfortably on the stool. How much do I really want to tell her? "Well, his name's Beckett."

"I like that. It's different."

Yeah, I should've figured that knowing how much my mom likes different names, hence Galileo and Star. A thought strikes me. "Hey, do you remember the band Killjoy?"

"Of course. I loved them."

"His dad is Barry Nash."

"Really? Your dad's gonna flip."

259

I prop my head up with my hand. "Dad liked them too?"

Mom nods, returning to the stove. "Is Beckett a musician like his dad?"

"Yeah, he is." I take a deep breath. "That's actually how we met. I sort of joined his band."

Mom whirls around, the spatula in her hand dripping on the floor. Recovering, she sets it down on the counter and reaches for a dishtowel. "You're in a band?"

"It's not really a big deal. We just practice once a week and play sometimes on the weekends. It doesn't take away from my studies, I promise."

"Why didn't you tell us sooner?"

I shrug, grimacing. "I wasn't sure how you'd take it."

Mom walks toward me. "Honey, you can tell me anything. You know that."

"But it just seemed like you didn't really want me to pursue music."

"I don't want you to give up your schooling for it, but I don't mind if you do it as a hobby."

"Thanks, Mom." Guilt washes over me for not telling her sooner, but I also feel relief that it's finally out in the open now. This must've been how Beckett felt when he finally shared about Quinn with me. It's hard to keep a secret trapped inside.

"What does Beckett play?"

"Guitar, and he's our lead singer." My lips push upward. "He's so talented, Mom."

"It sounds like you really like him."

"I do." *I may even be falling in love with him.*

Early Christmas morning, my phone trills. With my eyes closed and my head still pressed to my pillow, I reach out and run my fingertips over my nightstand until they flutter over my phone. Snatching it up, I press it to my temple. "Hello."

"Merry Christmas, Star."

I open my eyes and sit up in bed. "Merry Christmas, Beckett."

"I can't wait until you come back so I can give you my present."

"Does it involve scented candles and roses?" I tease.

"You have a dirty mind, Star Evans."

"It's your fault." I tuck an unruly strand of hair behind my ear.

"It is, huh?"

"Yeah, if you weren't so hot I wouldn't think like this so much."

"It is a curse for sure."

I shake my head. "So even Christmas isn't making you more humble, huh?"

Beckett laughs, and I long to be near him. I want to feel his arms around mine, his lips against mine.

"You're thinking about it again, aren't you?" Beckett says, and I hear the smile in his voice.

"Shut up." I giggle.

"Man, I love your giggle. I think I love it just as much as I love your singing."

I feel my cheeks warm. "I miss you."

"I miss you too. But it's only a few more days, and then you'll be back."

"I can't wait."

"Me either."

The couple of days after Christmas fly by in a whirlwind of shopping and hanging out with my family. They've wanted to know everything about the band and Beckett, and I've shared as much as I can. So far they're not being weird about it which is good. Dad's a little guarded, but he's always like that when it comes to me. I guess it's a dad's job or something. Beckett and I have talked and texted every day that I've been here, and I can't wait to go home tomorrow and see him in person.

After dinner I slip into my room and dial his number. Leaning against the wall I hold the phone to my ear.

"Hey, Star," Beckett answers.

"Hey." I slide down the wall and sit on the

carpet. Just hearing Beckett's voice makes me feel content. "I'm so excited I get to see you tomorrow."

"I know," he says, but his voice lacks its usual fire.

My stomach twists. "You okay?"

"Yeah. Why?"

"I don't know. You just sound distant or something."

"Oh, I just have a lot on my mind."

"Like what? Did something happen?" Agitated, I coil my hair around my finger.

"Sort of." He pauses. "We'll talk about it when you get back."

A sense of dread blankets me. I can tell by the tone of his voice that this isn't going to be a pleasant conversation. "Are we okay, Beckett?"

"Of course, Star."

I want to believe his words, but something isn't right. "Okay. I'll see you tomorrow then." I hang up, wondering if I'll be writing tortured lyrics again soon.

30
Beckett

"You're really going through with it, huh?" Tate gives me a curious look from where he sits on the recliner when I hang up with Star.

"I don't have a choice, man." I groan, dropping my cell on the coffee table.

"You always have a choice."

"Not this time." Just thinking of what I'm about to do causes my insides to churn. I lean my head back on the couch cushions and let a long stream of air push past my lips. Even though I know I'm doing the right thing, it doesn't make it any easier. I know it's going to rip my heart out of my chest to do it.

"I just don't think you should rush into anything, Beckett. Give it time. Talk it through with Star," Tate says.

I shake my head. "It's too late. I've already made my decision."

"It's just that you finally seemed happy for the first time in a long time."

"And this will make me happy too." I force a smile, hoping I'm right.

"I hope so." A weary expression cloaks Tate's face. "How do you think Star will take it?"

This is the part I don't want to think about. I had been so looking forward to Star returning to Seattle, but now I'm dreading it. After mulling over Tate's question for a minute, I answer honestly, "I think Star will take it the same way she takes everything. With grace and understanding." *And it's going to make me fall for her even harder.*

My stomach is in knots, and my chest is so tight I can barely breathe when I hear the knock on the door, signaling that Star is here. I glance down at her wrapped present sitting on the coffee table. I remember when I bought it and couldn't wait for her to open it. Now I'm not sure that it's going to matter at all. This day isn't going to turn into the heartfelt homecoming I had originally envisioned.

I barely have time to get the door open before Star is in my arms. I am assaulted with a rush of limbs, hands, lips, and her amazing honeysuckle scent. For one second I contemplate changing my mind. Perhaps being with Star is worth giving up everything for. I wonder if simply this would be enough for me. As her lips collide with mine and her hands massage the back of my head, I find myself fantasizing about what a future with her could be like. It's tempting, but the minute we part reality crashes over me and I know I can't afford to think like that.

"I missed you so much. " Star walks past me to get inside.

"Me too." I close the door, the weight of what I have to say bearing down on my shoulders.

Star sits on the couch, her gaze landing on the small wrapped box. Her eyebrows lift. "Is this for me?"

I plop down next to her. "Yes, it is."

She picks it up, rolling it in the palm of her hand. "It's a little too small to be roses and scented candles, huh?"

"Still can't get it off your mind, huh?" I grin, even though inside I'm dying. Bantering with her just makes this that much more difficult.

She nudges me with her elbow and giggles. Then she tears into the wrapping paper with gusto. I watch her flushed face with a growing sense of dread. There's nothing I want more than to take her in my arms and never let her go. I've never felt like this about anyone, and the thought of letting that go seems crazy to me. But then again, I don't believe in fairy tales. Just because I like Star so much now doesn't mean I always will. And what happens then? If I give up on this opportunity for her, won't I grow to resent her for it one day? That's a chance I just can't take. As Star reaches into the box with a pleased smile spreading across her face, my stomach knots. Why did I allow things to go this far? Why couldn't I be stronger when it came to her?

She pulls the silver necklace out, the star dangling from her fingertips. "Oh, Beckett, I love it!"

"Here, let me help you put it on." I grab the necklace from her hand.

Star turns around and pulls her hair away from her neck. It's a sensual move, and I swallow hard as her neck is exposed. My lips tingle and I want nothing more than to press them against her smooth flesh, but I hold back. Bringing my arms forward, I drape the necklace around her neck and fasten the back.

Star whirls back around to face me, her hand fluttering over the necklace. "It's beautiful."

"Not as beautiful as you," I say truthfully.

Her gaze lowers. "Well, my gift is going to seem stupid now." She reaches down by her foot and picks up the gift bag she had in her hand when she entered. "I didn't really know what to get you."

"Star." I place my hand over hers. "I'm sure I'm going to love whatever it is."

She takes a deep breath and thrusts the bag into my hand. I'm not used to getting gifts from girls, so it feels weird as I peel away the tissue paper and search for the gift at the bottom. My fingers brush over something that feels like a picture frame. I yank it out, and my heart sinks. It's a framed picture of Star and I singing together at the festival. We are so close our lips are almost touching. Only a single microphone is in our way. Our eyes are locked, our mouths open. The chemistry between us practically jumps off the picture. It's a reminder of what I'm giving up, and I feel bile rising in my throat.

"You hate it, don't you?" Star's small voice cuts into my thoughts. "I knew it was stupid."

"No." I grasp her hand. "I don't hate it, Star. I love it. That's the problem."

"Why is that a problem?" Her eyes betray her fear, and it kills me. It's like she knows what's coming, but she wants to avoid it. At this point I do too. I wish I didn't ever have to have this conversation with her.

After gently setting the picture down on the coffee table, I face Star. "I need to talk to you about something."

She nods, biting her lip. Her legs jitter nervously. I feel like the biggest jerk in the world.

"While you were at your parents' house I heard from a talent agent. He saw our set at the festival and loved it."

Her eyes widen, and the scared look from earlier starts to dissipate. "Really? That's awesome."

My insides coil into tiny knots at her expression. "Yeah, it is. He offered me an opportunity to go to LA and record a demo with him."

Star squeals. "That's amazing. We get to go to LA?"

"Not we, Star. Just me."

She freezes, cocking her head to the side. "I don't understand."

"He wants to just record me as a solo artist."

"Oh." Star smiles, but it doesn't quite reach her eyes. "Well, that's still great, Beckett. I'm so happy for you."

"I have to leave in a couple of days."

She nods, still forcing that damn smile. "How long will you be gone?"

I squirm in my seat. "That's the thing, Star. I don't think I'm going to come back."

The fake smile drops from her face. "What do you mean you're not coming back? Like ever?"

"Yeah. It just makes sense for me to stay. There's nothing really keeping me here."

"What about me?" The uncertainty in her voice kills me.

"You know that I care about you, but we've

only been dating a short time. This has been my dream my entire life. Can't you see that this is a once in a lifetime opportunity?"

"Of course, and I absolutely think you should do it. I just don't understand why you're going to stay there."

"I live in my brother's apartment. My parents want nothing to do with me. Everywhere I go, I'm reminded of the sister I lost. This is my opportunity to start my life over, Star. I can make something of myself in LA." I wish I could make her understand.

"What does this mean for us, though?" she asks.

This is the part I didn't want to get to. Slumping my shoulders, I give a resigned sigh. Star's eyes lock with mine and she nods slowly. "There is no *us* anymore, is there, Beckett?"

I bite my lip. "I didn't want things to end like this."

"Then don't end it." She rests her hand on my arm.

"I just don't see any other way." I stroke her fingers gently. "Long distance relationships don't work."

"They can." Her voice is so full of hope, and it cuts to my heart.

"You're only eighteen. I can't ask you to give up your life for me like that." I stare into her innocent eyes, knowing that soon another guy will be looking into them like this. The thought makes me feel sick, and again I wonder if I'm making a huge mistake.

"I guess I just thought I meant more to you than that." Her lips quiver, and her gaze darts away from me. She drops her hand from my arm. "Clearly I was wrong."

"No, don't do that." I reach for her. "Please, Star. You have to know that you mean a lot to me."

"No, Beckett. If I meant something to you then you wouldn't be leaving me so easily." She stands up, moving away from me.

"Damn it, this isn't about you. It's about my career, my life." I can't keep the irritation out of my voice no matter how hard I try.

She narrows her eyes at me. "You're right. I'm being selfish. You should absolutely take this chance. You deserve it." Reaching down, she grabs her purse with shaky fingers.

"Please don't be like this." I stand, a hard knot forming in my chest. This isn't how I want to say goodbye to her.

Her face is hardened, her lips a thin, straight line. "You should be proud of yourself, Beckett. You were so worried about me getting in the way of your dream, but you didn't need to be."

"Star," I breathe out the word, and grab her arm. She stiffens beneath my touch. "I didn't mean to hurt you."

"I know." Her voice is raw and clipped. "Good luck, Beckett. I really do wish you the best."

I squeeze her arm tighter, unable to let go. "Our goodbye can't be this way, Star. Can I at least get a hug?"

I sense her hesitation, but she slowly pivots in my direction. Drawing her to me, I circle my arms around her waist. She feels good in my arms, and it breaks my heart to know I have to let her go.

31
Star

I walk around in a daze the entire week after Beckett leaves. It's like I'm completely numb. The truth is I'm still in shock. The couple of days following our talk, I half expected him to show up at my dorm room and tell me he made a mistake. I totally understand his need to go make a demo album, but I just can't wrap my brain around the fact that he's never coming back. I thought we really connected. I thought we had something.

Going to classes and acting like nothing's wrong is brutal. All I want to do is curl up in a ball under my covers and never come out. I haven't heard from Beckett since the night I got back. Sometimes I wonder how he is, and what he's doing, but then I force myself not to think about it. Once my imagination starts running wild, I picture Beckett doing all sorts of things I don't want to.

Walking with clipped strides, I make my way across campus and head toward my class. I keep my head down and my jacket tight around my body. Wind whips into my face, and brushes over my hair. A few strands lift gently from my shoulders and spray over my cheeks. My boots click on the pavement under my feet reminding me of an uptempo drumbeat.

"Star," a familiar voice calls.

I turn around to find Ryker jogging in my direction, a backpack strapped on his back. "Hey, Ryker." The sick feeling returns to my stomach. Seeing Ryker always reminds me of Beckett, and makes me miss him even more.

"How are you?" His eyebrows are drawn together in a look of concern.

I lower my gaze. "Fine."

"I still can't believe he left. I mean, I know he liked you so much."

My stomach tightens. "I don't want to talk about it."

"Sorry." Ryker runs a hand nervously over his hair.

"It's not your fault." I fidget with the bottom of my jacket, rolling the soft fabric between my fingers.

"Hey, the guys and I are ready to start playing again whenever you are."

Ryker, Pierce and Jimmy had asked me to take over as the lead singer right after Beckett left. As tempting as it sounds, I'm not sure about it. "I know. I just don't think I'm ready yet."

"Fair enough." Ryker holds his hands out. "Let us know when you are."

"I will." I give him a tight smile before walking away. I wish the hard knot in my chest would loosen, but it seems to grow bigger with every step. When I reach my classroom, I heave a sigh of relief. I plop down in a seat near the back and unzip my backpack. Maybe if I focus on the lecture I can finally stop obsessing about Beckett.

"Hey, Star." A girl says breathlessly, taking the seat next to me.

I glance up. "Hey." Searching my brain I try to remember the girl's name. I only spoke with her one other time and it was the morning I joined Beckett. "Stacy, right?"

She nods, and then leans down to pull a notebook out of her backpack. When she sits back up, she peers over at me. "I heard about Beckett cutting a demo. Pretty exciting huh?"

Anger rises up in me, but I fight it down. "Yeah."

"I mean, I always knew he'd become famous one day, and now it sounds like it's gonna happen."

Biting my lip, I nod.

"I just wish I could've hooked up with him at least once before he left."

My head whirls in her direction, stunned by

her words. "What?" I can't keep the venom out of my voice.

Stacy's jaw drops, and her face reddens. "You two aren't like together, are you? I-I thought you were just in the band."

I sigh. "No. We're not together."

"Oh, okay. You kinda looked a little crazy for a minute there." She flashes me a relieved smile. "It's just that I've had a crush on Beckett for years, and I know he's not really the relationship type. Not that I care, I'd take what I could get with him. You know what I mean?"

I force my head to bob up and down, but inside I'm dying. If only I could make this girl shut up. When the professor starts his lecture, I give Stacy an apologetic smile and hunch over my notebook. She takes the hint and starts scribbling notes as well. Only I can't decipher anything the professor says. All I can think about is Stacy's words about Beckett. Was I an idiot to ever believe that I meant something to him?

"C'mon, Star, get out of bed. You stink." Lola swats at my covers with her hand.

I just groan and pull them further over my head. It's been two weeks since Beckett left, and each day seems darker than the last. No matter how hard I try to get over him, I can't. I think about him all the time, and it rips my heart open. I really think I was falling in love with him. I had allowed myself to start thinking about a future with him, and now that's all over. It's more than I can take right now.

"Star. You can't spend your life in bed." I feel her pulling on the covers, so I hold them tighter in my fist.

"Just go away, Lola," I say from under the safety of my comforter.

"No, this is ridiculous. You need to get up."

"Stop being so bossy." I stick out my bottom lip even though I know Lola can't see me. "You're not my mom."

"Well, you're certainly acting like a child."

All the anger that's been simmering just under the surface for years bursts out of me. I thrust my covers off and sit up. "Lola, I'm not a child. I'm an adult, and I don't need you to control my life anymore."

Lola backs up, looking stunned. "What are you talking about? I don't run your life."

"Yes, you do. You always have."

"Just because you're upset about Beckett doesn't mean you get to take it out on me." Lola brushes a strand of hair from her face. "If you remember correctly, I warned you about getting together with him."

"See." I point to her. "That's exactly what

I'm talking about. You're always telling me what to do. I don't need to be protected by you, Lola. I'm not the same girl you met freshman year. I'm capable of making my own decisions."

"Yeah, how's that working out for you?" She laughs bitterly.

I narrow my eyes at her. "That's not fair."

"Sorry." Lola plops down on my bed. "I just worry about you, Star. You're my best friend."

"I know." I reach for her hand. "And I love you for it, but I need you to back off a little."

"Look what happened when I did that?" Lola spreads her arms out. "You got your heart broken."

I smile sadly. "But I don't regret it. The times I spent with Beckett were worth it. They were some of the best of my entire life."

"Really?" Lola raises an expertly manicured brow at me.

"Really." I nod.

"I still can't believe he left you. Ryker's shocked too."

"I bet. I know the band isn't very happy."

"Well, he left everyone hanging."

I glance out the window of our dorm room, at the grey skies and thick clouds. "I know, but he's following his dream. He's doing exactly what he's always wanted to do."

"I hope it's making him happy," Lola says,

but it doesn't sound convincing.

There is a part of me that hopes Beckett is happy too, but I'd be lying if I didn't admit that there is a part of me that hopes he's as miserable as I am.

"Are you sure you don't want to go with us, Star?" Lola asks, throwing on her jacket. Ryker stands against the wall, one knee bent and his arms crossed over his chest. Even though he's had to wait forever for Lola to finish getting ready, he doesn't seem annoyed at all. I guess he is the right guy for my high maintenance best friend.

"I'm good here. I'm just gonna write some music or something."

Lola opens her mouth to protest, but then clamps it shut. Ever since our talk a couple of weeks ago, she's been working hard on not hounding me.

"C'mon, Star." Ryker pushes off the wall. "It will be good for you to go to open mic night. Pierce and Jimmy will be there too. Maybe we can all do a song together."

I know what he's trying to do. The guys have all been pushing me in regards to music. They're hoping I'll take the reins, and we can be a band again. Only I know it won't be the same without Beckett, and I just can't bring myself to do it.

"You guys just go and have fun. I'll be fine here."

"Are you sure, Star? It would be fun to jam together," Ryker says. "I know even Beckett wants us to keep playing together."

This gives me pause. "Have you talked to him?"

Ryker's face falls, and I can tell he regrets saying anything. "Yeah, I have."

"When?" My chest is so tight it hurts to breathe. I haven't heard from Beckett once since he left.

"We've talked several times, but the last time was earlier today," Ryker answers.

I bite my lip. "How is he?"

"Good. He's enjoying himself."

Lola shoots Ryker a sour look, but I'm grateful that he answered honestly. Maybe knowing that Beckett is doing well will help me move on. Right now it just makes me feel sick though.

"You okay?" Lola asks warily.

"Fine." I try to sound as chipper as possible. "You guys go have fun."

"Okay," Lola says with hesitancy in her voice.

"Bye," Ryker says, following Lola out into the hall.

The minute the door shuts I heave a sigh of relief. I know they are only trying to help, but sometimes I feel smothered. I just want to be left alone with my misery. Is that too much to ask? As I bend over and pull my keyboard out from under my bed, the star around my neck scratches my skin. It prickles, the sensation bringing a rush of emotions back. My mind travels to the memory of Beckett slipping it around my neck, and moisture fills my eyes. I blink back the unwanted tears and pick up my keyboard. After depositing it on my bed, I grab some papers and a pencil. I sit down cross legged and flick on the keyboard. Placing my hands on the white keys I press down, and music fills the silent room. Lately I've been favoring dark and haunting chords, and I think about how much Beckett would approve. This thought shoots a sick feeling into the pit of my stomach.

My cell buzzes. **Wish you were coming with us.**

I smile at Lola's text. Even when she's trying to back off, she can't do it. **Maybe next time,** I reply.

While I start to put the cell down, my thumb accidentally swipes across the touch screen and the texts scroll down. I catch sight of the last text between Beckett and me, and my stomach twists. My eyes connect with the words – the easy banter between us. I remember laughing when I received them. I remember thinking I was finally in a relationship that meant something. If only things had turned out differently. If only the talent agent could have taken us as a team, the way we wanted. Then maybe I'd be with him in LA.

I try to imagine what Beckett must be doing right now. I can picture him in his tight jeans, his guitar strapped over his shirt. He's probably out right now with a member of his fan club. It may be different than the one he had here, but I'm sure he's already got one. Beckett's charm draws girls to him like a magnet. Glancing down at my keyboard and blank papers, I curse myself for sitting at home alone on a Saturday night while Beckett is probably out with some slutty blond.

Frustrated, I stand up, brushing the crumbs off of my pajama pants. Guiltily my gaze lands on the empty bag of chips. Lola's right. I can't keep sitting around here feeling sorry for myself. Beckett may have left, but I have things going for me. I can be the lead singer of Beckett's old band. At least that will keep my mind off things.

I head to my dresser, and pull out a pair of jeans and a top. After changing quickly, I run the brush through my hair a couple of times and swipe lip-gloss over my lips. Then I grab my purse, and head outside. It only takes a few minutes to get to the coffee shop. The parking lot is full as always on Saturday night, so I end up parking along the street. As I exit my car, I wrap my jacket tighter around my body. The cold night air swirls around me, smelling of damp asphalt. My boots click on the pavement with each step.

I'm grateful when I get inside, and the warmth seeps into my fingers. I run my hands over my arms and wait for them to thaw. I spot Lola and Ryker sitting at a round table in the corner. They are deep in conversation, so I head to the counter to order my mocha. The sultry sound of a girl's voice belts from the stage. While waiting in line, I glance up at her. She sits on a stool, a guitar in her lap. Her voice isn't bad. A little too much vibrato for my liking, but she has potential.

"Hey, you made it." Lola sidles up next to me.

"Yeah." I shrug. "I figure it beats sitting at home."

"Well, I'm glad you're here. After you get your drink, come join Ryker and me."

"I will." I smile at her before she heads back to the table. When it's my turn, I head to the counter and order a large mocha. After getting my drink, I weave in and out of the tables until I get to Lola's.

"You gonna play?" Ryker asks after I sit down.

"I might." I grin, bringing the mug to my

mouth. Frothy foam paints my lips. I wipe it off with a small napkin and then it set it back down on the table. The girl on stage stops singing, and I hear her heels clicking on the stage as she exits. I take another gulp of my coffee, working up the courage to play. When I peer back up at the stage, my heart stops. *No way. What is he doing here?*

Beckett sits on a stool, his guitar in his lap. He's wearing his usual jeans and t-shirt. When his eyes lock with mine, I find it difficult to draw breath. I turn toward Lola, a questioning look on my face, but she looks just as surprised as I am.

"I want to play a new song tonight," Beckett says, yanking my attention back to him. "I wrote this song for someone very special; someone who changed my life. Someone who I thought I could walk away from, but I couldn't. Star Evans." He looks down at me pointedly, and heat creeps up into my cheeks. "I'm so sorry that I left. I thought that getting a recording contract and becoming a big star was all I wanted out of life until I met you. With you, I started to see that maybe there was more to this life than just being successful. Even so, when I got the opportunity to go to LA, I felt like I had to take it. I thought I would regret it if I didn't. But Star, once I got there the only thing I regretted was leaving you. Nothing mattered without you being there to share it with me." He takes a deep breath, and my eyes are glued to him.

I'm afraid to move or even breathe. "I love you, Star. I just hope I haven't screwed things up too bad between us." He strums his guitar. "I wrote this song for you."

Unexpected
You came along
I tried to fight it
But you're my song
What I was meant to sing
You're all I want
You're everything

Tears prick at the corners of my eyes as Beckett stands from the stool and hops off the stage, guitar still in hand. When he repeats the chorus one more time, his free hand finds mine and he helps me out of my seat, drawing me to him. I allow my body to be guided. His arm wraps around me just as he hits the last haunting note. His face nears mine.

"I'm sorry. Can you forgive me?"

I search his eyes and see nothing but sincerity. My head swirls. It seems like a dream. "Of course," I whisper.

He lowers his head and captures my lips in his. Cheers and clapping sound all around us. "I love you, Star," he speaks against my mouth.

My heart skips a beat at his words. I rest my hand against his chest, and breathe in the feel of him. "I love you too, Beckett."

After saying goodbye to Ryker and Lola, I follow Beckett out to his truck. My fingers are woven through his, and I'm squeezing so tightly my knuckles whiten. It's like I'm afraid to let him go. Now that he's back, I want to be near to him for as long as I can. Cold air stings my cheeks as we walk side-by-side. Once inside his truck, I rub my palms together in an effort to warm them.

Beckett slides in beside me and plants a kiss on my cheek. "Man, I missed you."

"Me too." I smile at him. "How long will you be back?"

"Forever."

I inhale sharply. "What?"

"I came back for good. I'm not going back." He scoots closer to me, laying his hand over my thigh.

It's what I wanted, and yet now that he's here I know I can't let him do this. I can't let him give up his dream for me. Placing my hand over his, I shake my head. "Beckett, you have to go back."

"No, I don't."

I sigh. "Since you left, all I've wanted is for you to come back to me."

"Then there's no problem." Beckett winks, flashing me a lopsided smile.

"Except that you're giving up your lifelong dream."

"When I first met you I was so worried that you would get in the way of my dream, but now I think that you're the only person who can help me reach it." He runs his fingers over my hand, causing chills to skitter up my arm. The windows around us fog up from the cold outside. At this point the parking lot is cleared out, and silence surrounds us. "My last night in LA I was in my hotel room, and all I could think about was how lonely I was without you. I realized that success wouldn't mean anything if I didn't have someone to share it with. I don't want to make it on my own. I want you there with me." He locks eyes with me. "And I think the two of us can make it together as a team. We're good together. Musically and otherwise." He flashes me a knowing smile that causes my stomach to flutter.

"So your fan club didn't keep you company, then?" I know I'm fishing, but I don't care. I need to know.

He kisses me swiftly on the end of my nose. "I wasn't with any girls in LA, if that's what you're asking. My heart belongs to only one girl now."

"And you have my heart fully and completely."

"Then I know I made the right choice."

I frown. "But I don't want you to ever resent me."

"I won't. I promise." Leaning forward, he presses his lips to mine. I latch on to him, my mouth moving in sync with his. In his kiss, I taste his passion and love. I respond back, surrendering to him. When we part, I lean my head against the window, my fingers tracing the tattoo on his arm. When I get to his elbow I catch sight of something new. I squint and move forward.

"Did you get a new tattoo?"

Beckett grins devilishly. "I was wondering when you'd notice." He holds out his arm, exposing his entire elbow.

My breath hitches in my throat. "It's a star."

"So you'll be with me everywhere I go." He steals a kiss on the inside of my neck, causing a wave of desire to shoot through my body. This whole night feels like a dream, and I seriously hope I never wake up from it.

"I love it," I tell him.

"We better get outta here. There's somewhere I want to take you," Beckett says, moving away from me. I nod, and sit back. After putting the key in the ignition, Beckett starts the truck and heads out of the parking lot. The streets are dark, the streetlamps casting an eerie glow on the asphalt in front of us. Since I'm still not very familiar with Seattle, I have no idea where we're headed. The only thing I can tell is that we're not going to the campus or Beckett's apartment. But I trust Beckett, so I settle into my seat letting the road rumble beneath me as he drives forward.

When he pulls over and stops the car, I glance up to see that we're at a cemetery. The iron gate looms before me, dark and imposing. My stomach twists, and I instinctually know why we're here.

When Beckett speaks, his tone is unsure and small. I've never heard him like that before, and emotion sweeps over me. "I've never come here, but I think it's time."

I reach up and stroke his face, my fingertips trailing over his light stubble. "Are you sure?"

He nods. "With you here, I can do this."

Together, we head out of the truck and make our way inside the cemetery. My feet crunch over the wet grass as I weave my way through gravestones. My gaze takes in the words carved into stones, the legacy of those who left the world behind. Some of the gravesites are littered with flowers, little balloons or stuffed animals. When we finally reach Quinn's, it's empty. Beckett kneels in the grass before hers, his knees dampening. I stand behind him, unsure of what to do. My arms sway uncomfortably at my side, and I turn my head away in an attempt to give him privacy. I'm startled when I feel his fingers brush over mine. His hand closes over my fingers, and he pulls me forward.

"Quinn," Beckett speaks into the still night air. "I want you to meet someone."

I step forward, and stand directly next to Beckett.

"This is Star," Beckett continues, his voice wavering a bit. "I wish you two could've met. You would've loved each other, I'm sure of it. You're very much alike."

I feel tears pricking at the corner of my eyes and my lips quiver a bit, so I bite down on them.

Beckett shakes his head, and I hear the regret in his voice. "Quinn, I'm sorry I haven't ever come to visit. I guess I just felt guilty about everything, but I'm done with that. I know you made your own choices in life, just like all of us. And I'm through being angry about it." I squeeze his cold fingers, urging him to continue. "I love you, little sis."

Swallowing hard, I blink back the tears that threaten to fall. Beckett stands, water staining his knees.

"You okay?" I ask him.

He nods, still staring down at his sister's grave. "I always wanted to come here. I thought it would give me closure or something."

"Did it?"

"Yeah, I think it sorta did." He turns to me,

taking both hands in his and pressing his forehead to mine. "Thank you, Star."

"For what?"

"For loving me. For helping me learn how to open up. For coming here with me."

"There's nowhere else I'd rather be."

"That's good, because I'm not letting you go. Ever." He brushes his lips over my cheek until they feather over my mouth and clamp down firmly. The rest of the world falls away as I lose myself in his kiss, his touch, his arms. I hold on tight, vowing to never let go.

Epilogue
Star

5 years later

Katie, my makeup artist, swipes gloss over my lips. I keep my face perfectly still with my lips pursed until she's finished. But that doesn't stop the nervous jittering of my legs as butterflies swarm in my stomach.

"Is it really packed out there?" I ask, a slight tremble in my voice.

"Are you kidding? The show sold out within the first day of the tickets going on sale," Katie replies while dusting powder on my nose.

"I can't believe I'm playing a sold out show."

"Are you really surprised? Your album has been number one for weeks." She puts the brush down and smiles at me. "Okay, you're all set."

A knock on my dressing room door startles us. Knowing who it is, Katie gives me a warning look. "Don't mess up your makeup."

I giggle. Her request will be difficult. "I'll do my best."

"Lovebirds." She shakes her head in mock disgust and goes toward the door. After opening it she slips outside, allowing Beckett to enter.

"Ten minutes to show time, Mrs. Nash."

I jump up from my chair and run into his arms. "I never get tired of hearing you call me that."

"And I never get tired of saying it." He lowers his lips to mine, and despite Katie's warning, I greedily kiss him.

"I can't believe this is really happening." I breathe against his lips.

"I knew it would. I always believed that together we'd make it."

"You're amazing, you know that?"

Beckett's arms tighten around me, and he winks. "Yeah, I know. You told me a million times last night."

I giggle. "Man, I married an egomaniac."

"Hey, it's a good thing that I know how to please my girl." He smiles, his gaze roving down to my skirt. "Speaking of which, think we can sneak in a quickie?"

"Oh, I wish." I lean into him, as his hands move down to my skirt.

"Five minutes," a loud voice bellows from outside my door.

I slump against Beckett and let out a sigh. "I think we better get out there."

He bends down and whispers in my ear, "Afterward then."

A quiver of desire runs through me. "I can't wait."

"Ready, Mrs. Nash?"

I nod as he links his fingers through mine. Glancing down, I catch the glint of my diamond wedding ring, reminding me of the vow I made to Beckett. My gaze lands on Beckett's wedding band, and I smile at the stars etched all around it. After giving my fingers an encouraging squeeze, Beckett guides me out of the dressing room. Together we head toward the stage. Just before we hit the stairs, Beckett turns to me. "I love you, Star."

"I love you too, Beckett. Always."

Want to read Ryker and Lola's story? Pick up LOVE STRUCK today!

Acknowledgements:

I truly have the best job in the world. I get to spend all day living vicariously through my characters, experiencing new things and falling in love over and over again. But even more importantly, I get to work with the most amazing people.

I have made so many friends in the book community - authors, bloggers, readers, fans, and I'm so grateful for all of you.

Thank you to:

My author friends - Megan Squires, Cambria Hebert, Cameo Renae, Alexia Purdy, Alivia Anders, Trish Dawson, Tara West, Melissa Pearl Gunn, Airicka Pheonix, all the authors in Indie Inked and many more!

My fabulous PA – Cassie Chavez. I am so appreciative of you!

My amazing street team!! Thanks for all your help!

All the bloggers and fans, my "adopted mama" Heather Andrews, and all those who read my books, I am truly grateful for you.

My betas - Megan Squires, Tiffany Tillman, Heather Andrews.

My family - Andrew, Eli, Kayleen, Mom, Dad, Karissa, Matt, Lindsay, Kagen, Brittnie.

My editor - Auntie Boo, you do such an amazing job!

My cover – Kris, you rock!
And to all my friends and family, thank you!!

A note to my readers:
First off, I want to thank you for taking the time to read this novel. I truly am honored that you took the time to read it.
Second, I want to invite you to contact me – either on Facebook, Goodreads, or my blog. I love to hear from my fans. It makes all this worthwhile. Also, you can join my newsletter if you want to be alerted to sales, cover reveals and release dates. Sign up here: http://eepurl.com/sp8Q9
Lastly, if you have enjoyed this book please help spread the word. Review the book on your blog, Amazon, Goodreads, Shelfari, Smashwords. Reviews really do help and I'm so appreciative of them! Also, mention the book on twitter and facebook. Any little bit helps.
Thank you and happy reading!